He was young and filled with adolescent dreams of purity and love —she was wise far beyond her years, and already marked by the bitter truths of life.

YOUR TURN TO CURTSY, MY TURN TO BOW

Here is a startling novel by that extraordinarily gifted young writer, William Goldman. It is his remarkable achievement to slash through the veils of forgetfulness and hypocrisy which are drawn over the passionate years of youth, and to reveal the truth with precision, clarity and sensitivity.

AN UNFORGETTABLE NOVEL BY THE AUTHOR OF *THE TEMPLE OF GOLD* AND *BOYS AND GIRLS TOGETHER*.

Also by William Goldman

*THE TEMPLE OF GOLD
†BOYS AND GIRLS TOGETHER

*Published by Corgi Books
†To be published by Corgi Books

WILLIAM GOLDMAN

YOUR TURN TO CURTSY,
MY TURN TO BOW

CORGI BOOKS
A DIVISION OF TRANSWORLD PUBLISHERS

YOUR TURN TO CURTSY,
MY TURN TO BOW

A CORGI BOOK

First publication in Great Britain

PRINTING HISTORY
Corgi Edition published 1966

Copyright © 1958 by William Goldman

Corgi Books are published by Transworld Publishers Ltd.
Bashley Road, London, N.W.10.
Made and printed in Great Britain by
Hunt Barnard & Co. Ltd., Aylesbury, Bucks.

For Tomine

YOUR TURN TO CURTSY,
MY TURN TO BOW

i

DURING THE SEMI-DISTANT DAYS that I can now refer to almost legitimately as my youth, I planned to write a book. Not just an ordinary book; no slap-dash hackwork ground out solely to entertain; not a philosophical diatribe; not an autobiographical outcry. No; mine was to be a giant, a titan, a great sprawling bitch of a novel crammed to overflowing with all the emotions, experiences, the joys and pains of Life itself.

I never got around to writing it.

For that I have Chad to thank. Chad Kimberley, who by trying to teach me so much taught me so little, and by teaching me so little inadvertently taught me so much. . . .

ii

ON AN EVENING in early June, some ten years ago, a young man sat nervously on the edge of his bed. Beside him lay a leather overnight bag, packed and ready. In his hands he held a baseball. Slowly he began to toss the ball from one hand to the other, right to left, then back, again and again, all the while looking around the room, from the desk, to the dresser, to the open closet door.

He brought the baseball to a halt and stared at it, turning it until the autograph came clearly into view. It said: "To Peter. Good luck from Joe DiMaggio." Rubbing the ball across his shirt, he began to repeat the tossing process, from one hand to the other, right to left, then back, again and again.

He heard his father calling him so he stopped. "Coming," he answered. Then, carefully placing the baseball inside the overnight bag, he zipped it shut. Again he heard his father's voice and again he shouted in reply.

"Coming. I'm coming."

He picked up the overnight bag and walked to the doorway. Then he set the bag down, surveying the room, checking one final time to see if there was anything he had forgotten. Finally satisfied, he took a deep breath, held it, and stopped, perfectly motionless.

And now as I look on that still figure, on the me of ten years past, as I look down through the darkening tunnel of three thousand days, I cannot smile. He embarrasses me. He fills me with regret. I regret the things he did, the things he did not do. I blush at his desires; I cannot share his dreams. The child may be the father of the man, but who is to insist that we must love our children.

How to describe him?

His name was Peter Bell and he was seventeen years old. Physically, he was big and clumsy, pimply-faced, neither as handsome as he wished nor as ugly as he feared. Mentally, he was bright, but not as bright as he secretly believed. He was indiscriminately virginal, a blank slate, a *tabula rasa*. But unhappily so. He desired nothing more than for the acid of experience to eat away at him, to burn some imperishable message on his imperishable soul. He wanted to taste of everything; he particularly thirsted after the world.

In other words, he was looking for trouble. Can there be any wonder that he found it...?

iii

"Coming. I'm coming."

Peter Bell hurriedly descended the circular staircase, dropped his overnight bag on the foyer floor, and walked down the three steps that led into the living room. Crossing the room, he approached his father who stood, hands clasped behind him, rocking, silently staring out of the picture window toward the bluff and the quiet lake beyond.

"I'm here," Peter said.

Jacob Bell turned and nodded.

"What do you want?" Peter went on. "The train doesn't leave for an hour."

"I thought we might have a talk."

"What are we going to talk about?"

4

"*We* aren't going to talk about anything. I'm going to talk. You're going to listen. Now sit," and he indicated the sofa with a short flick of his hand.

"O.K.," Peter said, sitting down. "What are you going to talk about?"

Jacob Bell pulled a wrinkled sheet of paper from his pants pocket and unfolded it, smoothing it with his hand. He stared at it a moment, reading. Then he shook his head and turned back to the window. "Christ, this stinks," he muttered. And, with his back still turned, "Have an apple." Peter reached out to the glass bowl set in the center of the coffee table and picked an apple from the top of the pyramided pile of red and yellow fruit. Stretching full length on the sofa, he looked up at his father.

Jacob Bell is shaped like a pear. Facially, he resembles Major Hoople of the comic strips. His legs are short, his feet tiny, his girth enormous, so that when he rocks back and forth, which he does continually, he gives the unmistakable impression of being about to topple over. He smokes nickel cigars, speaks like an immigrant, and it is a continual cause for wonder that such a funny little man should have risen from the Chicago slums to become one of the two or three most prosperous real estate men in the state of Illinois. Probably he is an immovable force, and it is doubtful that he will ever consent to die. But should he so decide, the conditions will certainly also be of his own choosing; perhaps in the card room at the country club after completing a triple schneider; perhaps in the bleachers at Comiskey Park when the White Sox have stoned the hated Yankees into submission. I cannot tell. All I can say is that in spite of his grammatical vagaries, in spite of his clown's face, he is the kindest and most gentle man I have ever known.

"I'm still here, you know," Peter said, a few minutes later.

Suddenly Jacob Bell whirled, a stubby finger pointing dramatically toward the ceiling. "God knows I have tried to bring you up decent," he said, his voice unnecessarily loud. His voice was always unnecessarily loud. "I have done my best as God is my witness. Is that the truth?"

"Yes."

"Thank you." He paused again, looking at the sheet of paper, rocking back and forth. "Now these are busy times for you," he went on. "Busy times. Yesterday you graduated high school. Today you're off on your first job. So I spent the afternoon jotting down a couple of things I figured I should tell you."

Peter Bell nodded, continuing to gnaw on the yellowing remnants of the apple core.

"As a matter of fact, there's probably a lot I can tell you. Many things. And now is as good a time as any to do it. It seems to me that way, at least. Do you agree?"

"You're stalling," Peter said.

"It's not so much that I'm stalling," Jacob replied, bringing the paper up close to his face, "as that this stinks so bad that I'm embarrassed to read it to you." He tilted the paper, squinting. "Anyway," he continued, "here I am, a whole life behind me, happenings both good and bad. And here you are, about to go out into the world and so ..."

"Come on," Peter cut in. "I'm not going out into the world. I'm just going to camp. For three months."

"Wrong," Jacob said, taking a black cigar from

his shirt pocket, striking a light off his fingernail. "After camp comes college. And after college, who knows." He stopped again, inhaling the cigar smoke, his eyes moving across the wrinkled sheet of paper.

"Do you want me to read it to myself?"

With a shrug, Jacob crumpled the paper and tossed it into the wastebasket. Then, his hands behind his back, the cigar jammed into his mouth, he began to pace the room. "All I'm trying to tell you is a couple of things you ought to know. That's all." He quickened his pace. "First, you must do what everyone tells you to do, but don't take any crap from anybody. Got that?"

"Got it."

Nodding, Jacob continued to pace, gesturing, mouthing words to himself. At the far end of the room he stopped. "Are you still with me?"

"You haven't said anything."

"Don't get wise. Patience is a virtue." He began jabbing his cigar into the air. "I got it." He snapped his fingers. "I got it. Now listen. Whatever happens to you, whatever it is, let it happen. Don't rush it."

"What do you mean?"

"I mean this. As you go through life, make goddam sure you go through life, and that life don't go through you." He paused, listening to what he had said. "That make sense?"

"I guess so."

Jacob started rocking again, smiling his clown's smile. "Then I'm finished. And together with a nickel that'll get you a piece of candy. Let's have a drink." He scurried to the bar. "Scotch?"

"Please."

Jacob nodded and busied himself at the bar. Keeping one glass, he handed another to his son.

Then he sat down on the end of the sofa. "How do you feel?"

"About the job?"

"About the job."

"Scared," Peter said.

Jacob nodded again. "Let's drink to that."

So they drank. And when they had finished it was time to leave. Peter walked up the steps to the foyer where Bertha and John were waiting for him. They had worked for his family since before he had been born and they met him in the foyer, Bertha handing him a box of cookies, John promising weekly reports on the perils of the White Sox. He thanked them, quickly picked up his overnight bag, and followed Jacob outside. Bertha and John stood in the doorway, calling his name, "Peter. Good-bye, Peter. Good-bye," waving to him. He turned and waved back and as he stared at the two of them, darkly silhouetted, their arms moving slowly, their voices calling his name, he began to feel that somehow time had slipped a notch, that it was again the Middle Ages, that he was setting off on some endless voyage to some distant Holy Land.

He and Jacob chatted during the drive to the Athens railroad station. Getting out of the car, they stood together on the platform. It was a beautiful Illinois evening, cool, with a promise of summer in the wind. They stood close together, waiting, until finally, off to their right, they heard the sound of the engine. Then a light flashed and the crossing gates closed.

Jacob Bell reached into his pocket. The sound of the engine grew, the outlines of the train taking shape, the light flashing across the track. "Here,"

Jacob said, and he jammed a fifty-dollar bill into his son's shirt pocket.

The train roared past them, slowing. "Thank you," Peter shouted. "But why?"

"Why not?" Jacob shrugged. "Why the hell not?"

"Thank you," Peter said again. "Thank you very much." The train stopped. A few cars to their left a shaft of yellow light knifed across the platform and a blue-coated conductor descended the steps.

Jacob Bell stood on tiptoe, kissed his son. "Have a ball," he muttered.

Nodding, Peter picked up his bag and ran toward the shaft of yellow light. Jacob stood quietly on the platform, his hands clasped behind him, rocking, rocking. Peter mounted the steps and waved. Jacob waved back. The train started up again, gathering speed. Smoke splashed between them. The train rounded a bend.

Peter gave his ticket to the conductor and followed along until they reached his drawing room. Closing the door, he sat on the bed and tucked the fifty-dollar bill into the card pocket of his wallet. He washed quickly, undressed, and turned out the overhead light. Picking up the baseball, he clutched it tightly for a moment, then put it back. He flicked off the bed light and lay propped on one elbow, looking out the window. Finally he lay flat, eyes open, his hands behind his head, staring into the darkness.

Today when I travel I travel by air. Trains are too slow for me. I find them uncomfortable. Their berths cramp me; their noises rob me of sleep. But they sang for Peter Bell. They drummed and laughed and rang and sang, and he understood them. The loose door banging on its catch, the great grinding wheels, the track, the cars; he understood them all. The thrust of motion thrilled him; the churning power of the wheels held him in awe. He understood them and they knew it and they sang all the louder for his understanding.

He listened....

iv

CAMP BLACKPINE CAMP FOR BOYS lies adjacent to the
town of Cherokee, which in turn is located on the
northern side of Lake Cherokee, one of the in-
numerable small bodies of water that serves to
smooth the otherwise rough face of the upper Middle West. The name Cherokee is a complete mis-
nomer; there is no record of any member of that
noble nation ever venturing into the area. How the
name came into being no one seems to remember.
In any case, it has survived, and just as well. Indian
names are highly valued in the state of Wisconsin.

Since the population is under two hundred,
Cherokee is an unscheduled railroad stop. Peter
Bell's arrival in town, then, created some small stir

among the few visible inhabitants. He jumped from the train before it had fully halted, stumbled, regained his balance, and waved once as the train picked up speed. Then he looked around.

The town of Cherokee consisted of a drugstore, a bar, a garage, a meeting hall, a post office, and a forked dirt road. Two old men sat on a sidewalk bench in front of the drugstore. Peter watched them for a moment, watched as their heads turned slowly toward one another, nodding, their lips moving silently. He brushed himself off and moved to the center of the dirt road, stopping, staring first one way, then the other. Finally the nearest of the two men raised a hand and gestured. Peter called "thank you," and followed the road as it led along the lake.

It was perhaps a quarter of a mile from the center of town to the camp entrance. Peter Bell walked quickly, kicking up small pools of dust with every step. To his left he was flanked by a row of giant pines, more than one hundred feet high; to his right by a row of small tourist cottages, with a few larger permanent homes standing guard in between. The lake front was dotted by short wooden docks, each with its own rowboat floating lazily beneath the midmorning sun. He walked faster, half running, his overnight case banging rhythmically against his leg. Then he was there. A large wooden arch spanned the road above his head. He looked up. On the arch was printed in flaking yellow paint CAMP BLACKPINE CAMP FOR BOYS. He walked through the arch.

A narrow trail snaked up a hill between a convention of small pines, and Peter followed the trail. At the top of the hill the ground leveled, and to his left he saw a cluster of white rectangular cabins, set flush with the earth. Directly ahead stood a large, brown-shingled house that he knew to be The Lodge. Running now, he bolted up the steps to the front porch, opened the screen door, put his overnight case in the foyer, and stopped, panting. From down the hall he heard the click of type-writer keys, so he tracked the sound until he stood in the doorway of the camp office.

A woman sat typing, her back to him, and he was about to say something when she spoke. "Be with you in a minute." Nodding, he waited, watching her. She typed extraordinarily well, so that the sound of the keys biting into the paper was almost a steady hum. Suddenly, with a single motion, she pulled the paper from the machine and spun around in the chair, facing him.

"Yes?" she said.

He walked into the room. "Hi," he began. "My name is Peter Bell."

"Yes," she said again.

He smiled at her. "I'm Peter Bell. I'm going to be a junior counselor this summer."

She nodded. "What is it you want?"

"I don't know exactly," he went on. "But I thought I ought to come here first. I just got off the train and I . . ."

"Didn't Granny meet you?"

"No. He didn't. Nobody met me."

"That's funny. He was supposed to."

"Well, he didn't. And I thought . . ."

"Of course," she interrupted. "Now I under-stand." He watched her as she stood and picked up a typewritten list, running her finger down the page. She was a short, bony woman, sharp-featured and plain. Her movements were quick, economic, without flair.

"You're to be in cabin number six," she said,

staring at the list. "You'll be able to find it easily. The cabins are numbered in order. You'll find your trunk in the rear. You can get it now and unpack." She glanced up at him. "Is everything clear?"

He shifted his weight from one foot to the other. "Not exactly," he said. "I don't understand. Where is everybody?"

"There's no one here now but Granny and myself. My name is Gert. I'm the secretary. Jeff is away. He won't be back until early Sunday morning. After you unpack you might go see Granny. He'll tell you what to do. If he has nothing for you, you can have the rest of the day to yourself. No one else is expected up until tomorrow." She sat down and quickly inserted some paper into the typewriter, her fingers hovering efficiently over the keys. Watching her, Peter wondered if she ever smiled.

"Well, thank you," he said.

She nodded. "You're quite welcome."

Slowly he returned to the foyer and picked up his overnight case. Then he located his trunk on the back porch, shouldered it, and, sweating heavily, his shirt sticking to his skin, he carried it across the lawn that separated The Lodge from the rest of camp.

Cabin number six was set on the edge of a small hill overlooking a pair of tennis courts. Peter opened his trunk, took out two sheets, and made his bed. Then he toured the cabin. It was divided into two rooms, a small, porchlike affair in front for the counselors, a larger square room in back, outfitted with four double-decker beds. Screens served as windows; a crisscrossing of two-by-fours between the overhead beams provided storage space. That was all. Peter was both surprised and disappointed;

he had expected more. For Camp Blackpine Camp for Boys was perhaps the most exclusive retreat of its kind in the Middle West. Certainly it was the most expensive; tuition for the full eight weeks ran well in excess of one thousand dollars.

Allowing the screen door to slam shut behind him, Peter began searching for cabin number one. He found it without difficulty. It was the largest of the cabins, located nearest to The Lodge. As he approached he was aware suddenly of sound and he stopped, closing his eyes, trying to place it. Finally he succeeded. It was the sound of heavy breathing, of great gasping inhales, explosive exhales, coming rhythmically from the cabin where Granny was. . . .

Granny Kemper. C. Granville Kemper. Of the Corset Kempers, as they were referred to in Athens. Granny's father was the owner of one of America's largest companies devoted solely to the manufacturing of foundation garments. Their most famous advertisement pictured a stunning brunette model hitchhiking. The caption read: "Want a lift? Get a Kemper!"

I knew him at that time only by reputation. We had attended the same high school, four years apart, and he was talked of still, primarily because of the measure of fame he had won by serving as blocking back for Chad Kimberley, both in high school and more recently in college.

I never cared much for Granny. There was one period, of course, when I hated him, but that did not last. I have never cared much for the company of confident men or confident women. There is something in their manner that seems to ferret out my most secret inadequacies, to display them for all to see. And Granny was confident, supremely so.

He acted as if somehow, when he was pulled wet and quivering from his mother's bloody womb, some secret voice had begun to whisper, "You are one of the chosen, you are one of the chosen, you are one of the chosen," again and again, until he had come to believe it, to accept it as a fundamental law of the land. . . .

Peter Bell walked into cabin number one and stopped. In the larger room beyond, Granny was lifting weights. He wore nothing but a pair of blue shorts slit up the thighs. A heavy metal barbell rested on his shoulders, and as he inhaled he practically threw it high over his head until his arms locked. Then, exhaling, he brought it down. Then up again, throwing it, then down, then up, and Peter could only stare. Granny had a magnificent body, broad, thick, incredibly muscular. The muscles in his chest were perfectly defined; his biceps bubbled as he brought the weight down to his shoulders. The entire cabin smelled of perspiration; it filled the air, clung to the window screens. Granny's body glistened beneath a film of sweat.

Finally he put the barbell on the floor and, feet wide apart, began shaking his arms, snapping them at the wrist, staring at his muscles as they rippled down, diminishing, disappearing through his fingers into the heavy air.

"What do you want?" he said.

"I was sent to see you. My name is Peter Bell and . . ."

"I know who you are. What do you want?"

"I don't know. Gert said I should come to see you. That you'd tell me what to do or whether I could have the day to myself or what."

"I've got nothing for you to do."

"Are you sure?"

Granny reached down and clamped his fingers around the barbell. "I said take off." He stood up and began curling, staring at the veins in his forearms as they grew taut, at his biceps as they swelled.

Peter left the cabin. As he walked away the sound of breathing followed him and the smell of sweat still clung to his nostrils. Wiping his arm across his nose, he broke into a run.

Back in his own cabin, he took the baseball from his overnight bag and lay down, tossing it up over his head, catching it, throwing it again. After a while, he sat on the edge of his bed and stared across the lawn at The Lodge. There was no one in sight, no movement, no sound of any kind. Putting the baseball away, Peter undressed and got into his bathing suit. Then, slinging a towel over his shoulder, he walked slowly toward the trail and followed it down the hill to the beach. The morning had warmed, the sky's blue deepened, and he began to hurry as he reached the bottom of the hill. Once there, he continued across the width of yellow sand to the camp dock, a mat-covered, wooden projection stretching fifty yards out into the lake. On the right side of the dock were a half dozen moored rowboats; on the left, a life-guard's tower; at the far end stood two diving boards, one high, one low. Next to the low board he saw a striped beach bag and beside that a large, white-tufted towel. But he did not see their owner.

Dropping his own towel onto the dock, Peter lay down, one side of his body brushing the edge of the high diving board. He clenched his fists, one above the other, and rested his head on top, staring out at the blue rippling waters of Lake Cherokee. Near the far shore a white sailboat floated into his vision, across it, then out of it again. Directly across the lake he saw a group of children splashing and yelling, but he could not hear them. He could hear nothing, nothing at all except the quiet slapping of the water against the dock.

Closing his eyes, he pressed his head down onto the flesh of his arms and fought off the desire to cry. He shut his eyes tighter, concentrating on it, until even the slapping of the water receded. Then he heard a voice from somewhere above him.

"Lookout!"

He did not move until the voice came again.

"Lookout if you don't want to get splashed."

Peter rolled over and opened his eyes.

Tillie Keck was standing on the high board, her hands gripping the guard rails, staring down.

v

A PROFESSOR OF MINE once gave me some advice that I have never been able to forget. I had just written a play, not a bad play, or so I thought at the time, in which I had employed that most anachronistic of theatrical devices, the soliloquy. The professor, his name is forgotten, was gently critical of my efforts, touching on this point and that until he came to the soliloquies. He asked me what I thought of them. I replied that I felt them to be just a shade below brilliant. He nodded. And then he said this: "Bell," he said, "when you get someone out there to say something, make sure he has something to say."

Forewarned is forearmed. I would now like to talk about beauty.

Beauty . . . ? What? Beauty is only skin deep?
True. Beauty lies in the eyes of the beholder?
Again, true. A thing of beauty is a joy forever?
Endlessly true. But it has all been said before. So
it should be sufficient merely to state that Tillie
Keck was a beautiful girl. Still, that in no way
explains the effect she had on Peter Bell. He had
seen other beautiful women; gliding from limou-
sines into restaurants; standing model-like in theater
lobbies; caressing their bodies with oils beside the
country club pool. Perhaps it was the way he first
saw her, looking down on him from the high diving
board, materializing suddenly, as if some wizard
had shaped her and placed her there solely for his
benefit and pleasure, to brighten what had been a
lonely morning at the start of a lonely summer.
First glances meant a great deal to Peter Bell. He
had once spent a college week end with an unde-
niably attractive Radcliffe sophomore. He never
thought her attractive, however, primarily because
when they first met, in a Schrafft's near the Times
Square area, her mouth was full of chicken salad.
Whenever he looked at her from then on, he kept
seeing her tiny mouth opening and closing on a
brownish combination of celery, chicken, and may-
onnaise.

But Tillie Keck was beautiful. Tall, perfectly
formed, she was blessed with gently curling auburn
hair, skin as clear as autumn snow. She was exquisite, and not to his eyes alone. For on the afternoon of the day they met, as they were strolling
through the town of Cherokee, an old man, perhaps
the same old man who had gestured to Peter that
morning, stopped them, blocking their path. Then,
without a word, he slowly raised an aged freckled

hand and, trembling, softly touched his fingers to her skin. ...

"Lookout," she called again. "You'll get splashed."

"Go ahead," Peter answered, getting to his feet, moving away from the board.

"Lookout below," she said. "Here I come."

"Go on," and he stared up at her. "I won't get wet."

"O.K.," she muttered and she walked to the end of the board and turned around. "Here I go." She rose up on tiptoe, balancing herself, getting ready for a back dive. "Now inhale," she went on. "Now relax. Now ..." She dove off the board. Her body arched momentarily, then straightened, and she landed flat, spraying water in all directions.

Peter ran to the edge of the dock and watched as she floated, groaning audibly. "Are you all right?" he called.

She ducked under and came up by the ladder, pulling herself hand over hand, muttering all the while. She walked past him to the high board and mounted it again. "How'd that look?" she called, when she stood on top.

"Not very good," Peter answered. "Like it hurt."

She nodded and walked to the end of the board and turned around. "Now inhale!" she said, more violently than before. "Now relax! Now ...!" Again her body arched out over the water, but this time it did not straighten and she knifed into the lake, legs together, toes pointed. She swam to the ladder and pulled herself up.

"Better?"

"Yes."

"Good." She folded the large white towel around her body, jumping up and down, clearing the water from her ears.

Peter watched her. "Do you like to dive?" he asked.

She shook her head. "I hate it. My back's still sore. I'll kill myself on that goddam board."

"Why do you do it, then?"

"It's good for the bodily control. Like ballet dancing." She dropped the towel by the beach bag and walked over to him, holding out her hand. "I'm Tillie Keck," she said. "Who're you?"

He told her who he was.

She gestured. "At the camp?"

"Yes. I'm going to be a junior counselor this summer. I just arrived this morning. It's my first day. I'm sure glad to see you. There's nobody to talk to around here. I've never been up here before. Do you like trains?"

"What?"

"Oh, it's just that I like them and I wondered if you did. I didn't mean anything by it. Nothing important. But I love riding on trains. I suppose I like riding on trains as much as I like anything. I just . . ." and he chattered on, his eyes focused on her eyes, until she turned and knelt by the beach bag and took out a book and an alarm clock. He was still talking when she came back. Then he stopped.

"You going to be here awhile?" she asked.

He nodded.

"You want to do me a favor?"

He nodded again.

She sat on the edge of the dock and motioned him down beside her. Putting the book in her lap, she was quiet a moment, staring at the alarm clock, her lips moving. Then she handed him the clock and stretched out on her stomach, resting her chin in her hands. "It's now seven after eleven," she told

22

him. "Let me know when it's fourteen after." Then she began to read.

"Where are you going at fourteen after?" Peter asked.

She glanced up from her book. "I'm not going anywhere. I have to turn over then."

"Oh," he said, and he looked at her as she lay alongside him, her lips moving silently, her auburn hair shifting softly in the wind. "Why do you have to turn over?"

"To tan even," she answered, her eyes still on the book. "Why did you think?"

"I didn't know," he said. "So I asked." He paused. "I always do that." She nodded and went on reading. He stared at her, trying not to breathe. "But why do you have to tan evenly?"

"Aw, come on," she muttered, dropping the book. "How'm I going to read? I'll talk to you when I'm on my back. I can't read then. The book blocks the sun."

"I'm sorry." He forced his eyes to the alarm clock, watching the small second hand tick around. "It's eleven fourteen," he said, when it was.

"Thank God," she muttered, and tossed the book aside. Carefully she rolled over, pointing her toes, angling her body toward the sun. She closed her eyes. "Tell me when it's seven minutes."

"Yes," he said. "I will." He pushed himself up on one elbow and watched her. She was wearing a white bathing suit, and the color stood in gentle contrast to the golden texture of her skin. Her breasts rose lightly as she breathed, pressing against the soft white fabric of the bathing suit. Her legs were long, round, and golden. Peter held his breath.

"I thought you wanted to talk," she said, her eyes still closed.

23

"Oh, I do," he answered quickly. "I'd like that very much." He exhaled. "Why do you have to tan evenly?"

"Because it's important, that's why."

"Yes," he nodded. "I see." And then: "Do you work up here?"

"I'm what you might call on vacation," Tillie answered. "My aunt"—she pronounced it "awnt"—"my aunt is secretary at the camp." She gestured blindly with her thumb.

"Gert?"

Tillie nodded.

"I met her this morning. She seemed very efficient."

"She is. She even goes to the bathroom on schedule."

"I wouldn't know about that," Peter said. "But she types very well." Across the lake two sailboats were racing, and he watched them cut into the wind. The children he had seen earlier were gone, and the entire lake seemed deserted except for the two boats knifing through the blue water, their white sails puffed full. "What are you reading?" Peter asked.

"It's some crappy thing on manners. Etiquette, it's called."

"Why are you reading it if it's so bad?"

"Because it's important."

"Why is it important? What's so important about it?"

She opened her eyes. "You sure like asking questions, don't you?"

"Yes," he muttered. "I do. I always like to know what's going on. I'm sorry." He lay flat on the dock and put the alarm clock on his stomach, staring

24

at it. The breeze seemed suddenly stronger; the sun flamed steadily above them.

"What's an outside spoon?" Tillie whispered, breaking the silence.

"I'm sorry," Peter said. "I didn't hear you."

"An outside spoon," she repeated. "What is it? It says in the book that you should always start eating with the outside spoon. I didn't know what it meant."

"Well," Peter began, "at a dinner party, you always eat the first course with the spoon that's on the outside. Farthest to your right."

"You mean there's more than one?"

"Oh, yes. Sometimes three or four or five. It all depends on what you're having, how many courses and all."

"Five spoons," Tillie said softly. "Have you ever been to a meal like that?"

"Yes. But I don't like them much."

"Five spoons," she whispered. "God, would I love to eat at a meal with five spoons." She opened her eyes and looked at him. "Is it time?"

Peter picked the alarm clock off his stomach and set it on the dock. "Yes, it is."

Tillie rolled over and cupped her hands around her chin, turning the pages, trying to find her place.

"What's the point of all this?" Peter asked her. "Why?"

"I'm practicing."

"What are you practicing for?"

"To be a world-famous celebrity," Tillie told him. And then she began to read. . . .

"Are you going to sun yourself much longer?" Peter asked. It was well after twelve, and they had been talking intermittently for more than an hour.

"Until it's one o'clock. I always stay here from eleven 'til one. The rays are the strongest between then."

Peter sat up and nodded. "I know we've just met," he began, his tone violently casual. "I realize that. And of course I don't mean to be gauche, but..."

"What does it mean?" Tillie interrupted. "That word?"

"Gauche?"

She jumped to her feet and hurried over to the beach bag, reaching inside, bringing out a pencil and a small brown notebook. Then she came back and sat beside him, turning the pages of the notebook for a moment. Finally she stopped and licked the end of the pencil with her tongue. "O.K.," she said, "shoot."

"It means clumsy," Peter began. "Tactless. Awkward."

"Which does it mean most?"

"All of them."

Muttering, she looked at him. "Spell it."

"G-a-u-c-h-e. Gauche."

Carefully, mouthing each letter, she printed the words into her notebook. Then she looked up, smiling. "That's a good one," she said, flipping the pages in front of him. "I got pages full of good words in here. Every day or so I read them over. That's the best way to learn them."

"*Pygmalion*," Peter said.

"What?"

"*Pygmalion*. It's a play by George Bernard Shaw. About a speech teacher who finds a girl and teaches her how to speak correctly. Then he takes her to a very spiffy ball and passes her off as a duchess, and no one catches on. It's a terrific play. You ought to read it."

She nodded and reopened the notebook and wrote for a moment. "I got the Pig part," she said then. "How do you spell Malion?"

Peter burst out laughing. "It's not P-i-g, it's P-y-g. And it's not two words. It's one. *Pygmalion.*"

"Stop that laughing!" Tillie said.

"I'm sorry," Peter answered quickly. "I didn't mean anything by it. I'm sorry. Honestly. I am."

She jumped to her feet, throwing her belongings into the beach bag, slinging it across her shoulder.

"I apologize," he said louder. "I'm sorry. I was gauche then. That's what it means."

She started walking slowly down the dock.

"Please," he called. "Please don't go."

She stopped. "I got a terrible temper," she muttered, turning. "I should have told you earlier."

Peter stood. "No. It was all my fault, but what I meant was pardon me for being gauche but can we have lunch together?"

She giggled suddenly. "I know a joke about that."

"Please. I mean it. Will you?"

"Where?"

"In town. There must be someplace to eat in town."

"There's a drugstore I guess. I haven't been in much."

"Well?"

She thought for a moment. "You paying for it?"

"Of course. Yes."

She smiled at him. "Then sure."

"Great," Peter said. "Great. Terrific. But I've got to get my money. I'll meet you back here. In ten minutes. Back here." With that he grabbed his towel and ran past her and bolted up the hill.

"Cookies are my heart's desire," Tillie was saying. "Can I have some more?"

"Sure," Peter nodded.

They were sitting at a table in the corner of the Cherokee Drugstore, finishing lunch. He waved to the old woman behind the counter. "More cookies, please." She threw a small, cellophane-wrapped package over the counter; he reached out and caught it.

"When I die I hope it's eating cookies," Tillie went on, unwrapping the cellophane, nibbling slowly at the corners of a chocolate graham.

Peter watched her. She was wearing a white sleeveless blouse and a green skirt and her auburn hair fell lazily across her shoulders. "Why is that?" he said.

"You sure like asking questions, don't you?"

He nodded. "I told you. I always like to know what's going on. It's a habit I have. I can't break it, no matter how hard I try. Personally, I don't care much for cookies. Why do you?"

Tillie looked at him a moment. "It'll sound simpy," she began. "But it's just that my mother used to make cookies at Christmas time. Batches and batches of cookies. All of them the same kind. Checkerboard. God, but I love checkerboard cookies. When I was a little kid, I used to sit in the kichen and spread a whole mess of checkerboard cookies in front of me and then I'd count the squares. There were always nine squares to each cookie. I remember that. Nine. But I'd never eat them. No matter how much I wanted to, I'd never eat them. I'd just take them out and count the

28

squares. They used to last for a month that way, maybe longer." She stopped and closed her eyes. "Crap," she muttered, and finished the chocolate graham.

"Would you like some more?" Peter asked. "For this afternoon?"

She shook her head. "I can't. I got to watch my figure. I count calories very carefully. I know how many calories are in almost anything you can name. It's a knack I have." She started nibbling on another cookie.

"That must come in very handy," Peter said.

"It does. Calories and movie stars. They're my two best subjects. I know everything about Greta Garbo, for instance. Everything. And Clark Gable. I know all about him too." She waved her hand. "It's just a knack." She finished eating and they got up, Peter paying for lunch, opening the door for her. She brushed against him as she walked past, her green skirt swirling around her long tanned legs.

When they reached the sidewalk, they stopped. An old man stood in front of them, blocking their path. Peter stepped around him and Tillie was about to follow when he reached out for her. Without a sound, he touched the tips of his fingers to her skin, running his freckled hand along the gentle curve of her cheek. Then he dropped his hand, stepping aside to let her pass, staring at her as she walked by.

Peter fell into step with her, and they had reached the lake and taken the turn along the dusty road toward camp before he realized that she was crying.

He reached out quickly for her hand but she twisted free. "Getaway," she said.

"He didn't mean any harm, Tillie. It's nothing to cry about."

She shook her head, continuing to walk, faster than before.

He hurried along beside her, keeping step. "I wish you'd stop, Tillie. Please." She was half running by then, kicking up dust, coughing. "You shouldn't mind," Peter said, his voice louder than he meant it to be. "You shouldn't. Don't you understand? That was a compliment."

She whirled on him. "You think I don't know that? I get lots of them. All the time. My stepfather tried to rape me when I was sixteen. That was my first compliment."

"I'm sorry," Peter muttered.

"Sorry! You are the simpiest kid. You're sorry. How do you think I felt?"

"How did you feel?" Peter said. "I'd like to know."

She paused, breathing deeply, studying his face. "You really would, wouldn't you?"

"Oh yes," he answered. "It sounds very interesting. I'd like hearing about it. Very much."

Tillie ran her tongue across her lips. Then she started walking again slowly. "Scared," she began. "That's how I felt. It was the scariest thing ever happened to me." She glanced sideways at him, and he nodded to her, waiting. "It's no big secret or anything," she went on, her voice soft. "Anyway, all my life I'd been tall and skinny. A beanpole. Then, when I was sixteen, I guess I blossomed. You understand?"

Peter nodded.

"Well, one day I was upstairs taking a shower when all of a sudden I heard the toilet flush. So I looked out, and who's there but my goddam stepfather, smiling at me. 'How you doing?' he says. 'I was doing fine,' I tell him. 'Don't let me bother you,' he says. So I ask him to please get out and I go on with my shower. I knew he was potted from the way he smelled and I didn't much want to argue with him. And then I saw he's still there. We had one of those white shower curtains you could see through, shapes and like that, and he's staring at me through it. I was never so scared in my life. And the next thing I knew, he's ripped away the shower curtain and there he is and there I am. 'Let's have a little talk,' he says. I told him to get away but he came for me anyhow and tried grabbing me. But I was wet and I guess slippery and I pushed him backwards over the toilet seat and took off out of the bathroom, him in hot pursuit. He cornered me in the kitchen and started chasing me around the kitchen table, around and around, the both of us screaming. I grabbed up a frying pan and raised it over my head. And I said, 'You come one step closer, you polack bastard, and I'll brain you with this frying pan.' Then he came for me."

"What happened?" Peter said. "What happened?"

Tillie shrugged. "I brained him. All I had. Smacko! Right on the head. He went out like a light, flat on the floor. I was standing over him with the frying pan still in my hand when in walks my mother. 'And what's been going on here?' she says. 'Your husband just tried to rape me,' I tell her. She dumped some water on his face and he came to.

"It was a whale of an evening. Everybody yelling at everybody else, telling them where they can head in. And the upshot of it all was that my mother sent me to live with my Aunt Gert. She told me, 'Tillie,' she said, 'you're a good kid and all that but you gotta get out. I can always have another baby, but a husband's tough to find when your looks are going.' So I left."

"You're kidding," Peter said.

"God's truth," Tillie answered. "I've spent the last two years with my Aunt Gert. She hates me. She figures that just because my mother got pregnant before she got married, that makes me no good. Her and her efficiency. She really hates me, Gert does. I'm a milestone around her neck."

"Millstone," Peter said. "Not milestone. Millstone."

Tillie stopped walking and turned, staring up at his face. Peter smiled. He meant a great deal by that smile, and probably she understood, at least some of it. Because laughing out loud she threw herself into his astonished arms. . . .

It was a magnificent afternoon. The air was warm for early June, and as the hours passed it lingered warm. The sun moved clearly across the deep blue sky, unhampered by clouds; cooling gusts of wind blew occasionally across from the far side of Lake Cherokee.

But it was not the weather that so appealed to Peter Bell. And it was not the conversation he had with Matilda Keck of Baraboo, Wisconsin; a conversation that ranged aimlessly, unencumbered by direction. It was looking at her that did it. Just looking at her. Standing, sitting, walking around her, glancing at her from the side, from the front, almost hopefully trying to find some flaw lurking hidden in her flawless face. He found none. She was perfectly beautiful. Everything about her was beautiful. Her toes were beautiful, her knees were beautiful, her elbows, her ears. Her tanned legs were beautiful, her mouth, her incredible eyes. Her shoulders were broad and beautiful, her waist narrow and beautiful, her hips curved beautifully, her breasts rose beautifully as she breathed. And there were times, many times as he furtively glanced at her sitting beside him, that he wanted nothing more than to scream out loud for sheer unadulterated joy. Her skin was beautiful, perfectly clear; her arms were round and beautiful, her fingers slender and tapering, and oh God he thought she was beautiful. She was perfect, she was stunning, she was exquisite, she was . . . Oh yes, she was.

They spent the afternoon together on the lake front, skipping stones from the beach, sitting on the dock, staring at the white sails across the water, talking, talking, sitting quietly, then talking again, and probably he fell in love with her that afternoon. Of course, he was never certain, then or later, if he really was in love. "No" was his answer later. "Yes" he would have said then.

So it was a magnificent afternoon. At least until Granny came.

They were sitting close together, staring out at the sun as it dropped exhausted behind the pine forest at the west end of the lake, when from behind them they heard a car horn honking. Tillie jumped to her feet and brushed off her skirt.

"I'll be seeing you," she said. "So long."

"What are you . . ." Peter began, turning. Then he stopped. Granny was sitting in a red convertible beneath the Camp Blackpine Camp for Boys sign, his fist pounding repeatedly on the horn.

Tillie started down the dock. "Wait a minute,"

Peter called, and he ran after her. "Are you going out with him?"

"Yes, I'm going out with him."

"Well, you shouldn't."

"Mind your own business," she snapped. "What do you think you are?"

"O.K.," Peter muttered. "Go on. See if I care."

He stood motionless, watching as she hurried down the dock, across the beach, into the car. Granny jammed the gears into reverse, turned, and the car shot forward with a roar. Peter stared after them, still not moving, until they were gone. Then he cupped his hands over his mouth. "You shouldn't have gone with him," he shouted. "You should have stayed with me," and from across the lake an echo picked up his words and threw them back at him, "with me." Then, fainter, "with me." Then there was no sound.

Peter walked to the low diving board and climbed out on it, lying flat, pressing his stomach down hard on the board, his arms dangling loosely over the water. The matted covering hurt his face, so carefully he turned and lay on his back, staring up. "How the hell could she?" he shouted again, but this time there was no echo. "Goddam Granny," he shouted. "Goddam musclebound fatassed fool of a Granny." He pressed his hands down onto his eyes until he saw the explosions of white beneath his lids. "She's beautiful," he cried. "She's beautiful. She's . . ." He stopped and raised his head, looking around, making certain he was alone. "Beautiful," he finished finally. He turned his voice across the lake, shouting, "Beautiful. Beautiful. Beautiful," and then he lay back quickly and closed his eyes, listening to the dying of the echo.

The moon was rising and the air seemed suddenly cooler. Peter rubbed his hands along his arms, feeling the goosebumps. He swung into a sitting position, his knees over the side of the board, his toes almost touching the water. He realized it was suppertime, but he felt no hunger, so, standing, he shoved his hands into his pockets and ambled down the dock to the beach, following it. At the end of the beach he struck off into the woods.

Camp Blackpine Camp for Boys had been founded eight years before by Jeff Jeffers. No one remembered his Christian name; universally he was Jeff. The money necessary to start the enterprise, as was generally known, came from the Kempers. Mr. Kemper and Jeff had chosen the site themselves, after a month of driving through Minnesota, Wisconsin, and the northern peninsula of Michigan.

They had chosen well, Peter realized as he walked along, feeling his moccasins sink into the soft layer of pine needles that blanketed the earth. He moved slowly, parallel to the lake, his hands still in his pockets. Every so often he stopped and breathed deeply, filling his lungs with the rich pine-scented air that permeated the wood. Above the yellow moon climbed, accompanied now by more stars than he had ever seen before. They flooded the sky, dotting it with soft specks of white light. All around him rose the giant pines, the smaller black birch, blocking his way, so that he was continually forced to sidestep, backtrack, before moving ahead. Through the trees to his left he saw the lake, shimmering, covered with soft yellow light. Everything seemed soft to him; the pine needle floor of the wood, the sky, the moon, the yellow-topped lake; they all seemed to meld and melt into a great taffy-textured landscape, with only the bare-trunked trees serving to shatter the image. He ambled on.

He had no idea of time, or place, but only of soft things, of water and sky and thick-carpeted earth.

It was then that he found the clearing.

A hidden place, tucked behind a clump of birch, set at the entrance to a small cove in the lake. He walked to the edge of the clearing and looked down at the water some twenty feet below him. Then he turned his back on it and stared around the clearing. It was small and circular, no more than ten feet in diameter, with a tree stump in the center. The ground was particularly thick, and as he paced the perimeter his moccasins kept getting caught, so he took them off, his socks too, and walked barefooted around and around.

He had approached the stump and was about to sit down when he saw the initials. It was not light enough to see them clearly, so he traced them with his finger. "C" was the first letter. Then "K." "CK." He thought a moment. Chad Kimberley. Chad Kimberley must have been here once. But years before. The initials were old. Peter sat, back against the stump, staring out at the water. Finally he lay flat, his hands behind his head, and for a time he counted the countless stars. His eyes felt suddenly heavy. The air was warm, the wind gentle. He took a deep breath, his eyes closing.

And so the first day ended, a day that he knew, even then, he would not be able to forget. For he had found an enemy; and he had made a friend. . . .

vi

THE SUN WOKE HIM. With a start he tried to rise, but his back was stiff, as he lay flat a moment and stretched, yawning, rubbing the sleep from his eyes. It was another beautiful day, clear, cloudless, and the morning air smelled richly of pine. Slowly, pushing himself to his feet, he began to thread his way through the woods toward camp.

He got to cabin number six a few minutes later and immediately undressed, tucked a towel around his waist, and hurried to the latrine. He shaved quickly, showered, returned to his cabin, threw on some clothes, and ran across the lawn to The Lodge.

Granny was sitting on the front porch railing, his thick arms crossed in front of him. He was wearing a tight pair of khakis and a T-shirt with the sleeves ripped off. Peter walked up the porch steps and halted, returning Granny's stare. It was then that he first noted, with undisguised pleasure, that Granny's hair was thinning badly on top, that, even at the age of twenty-two, the hairline had begun to recede.

"Where the hell have you been?" Granny said.

"I fell asleep out in the woods. I guess I was tired. I overslept."

"You're a real nature lover, aren't you, buddy boy?"

"No. I was just tired."

"Get tired on your own time. You're up here to work." He began pounding one hand into the other, the right into the left, again and again.

"I wanted to talk to you about that," Peter said. "I was wondering. I wondered. Could I work down at the waterfront?"

Granny looked at him a moment, then laughed out loud. "Why?"

"No special reason."

"If there's no special reason, then you can't work down there."

"Come on," Peter said. "Come on, please. Let me. There must be something I can do."

"Why do you want to work down there?" Granny repeated. Peter said nothing. "Tell me," Granny went on, pressing it. "Tell me why."

"Because of her," Peter muttered. "Because of Tillie."

Granny laughed again, louder. "Oh, the girl," he said. "That's a good enough reason. You want to keep her company, is that it?"

Peter nodded.

"O.K., then. I'll let you work down there."

"You mean it?"

"Sure, buddy boy. I mean it. Get some green paint from the shed out back. Paint a couple of canoes. And keep her company all at the same time. That what you want?" He walked down the steps to the cement walk.

"Thank you," Peter said.

"Don't mention it," Granny answered, not turning. "Pleasure's all mine."

Peter watched him until he was out of sight. Then he opened the screen door and entered The Lodge.

Gert was typing at her desk. "Good morning," Peter said.

She spun around in her chair. "What did you say?"

"Nothing. Just good morning."

"Yes," she nodded, and resumed typing.

With a shrug, Peter left her and followed the hall to the kitchen. He made himself breakfast, gulped it down, cleaned off his plate, and hurried out to the paint shed. Grabbing a can of green paint and a wide, stiff-bristled brush, he half ran back to cabin number six and put on his bathing suit. Then he headed for the lake.

There was no one else there. He stared along the beach, out onto the dock, into the water. He was alone. Nervously he dragged a canoe across the sand, lifted it, and turned it upside down on top of two wooden horses. Glancing continually over his shoulder, he began to paint.

It was shortly before eleven o'clock when Tillie Keck made her appearance, wandering out onto the dock, beach bag in hand. Peter watched as she climbed up on the high board and lay down. A few minutes later she stood, walked to the end, hesitating a moment, finally diving in. The second time, she attempted a back dive, repeated it, then began drying herself with the large white towel.

Peter called to her, waving. She looked around, saw him, and waved back. Then she stretched out and began to read. Peter dropped the brush into the paint can and walked onto the dock.

"Good morning," he said.

"Good morning." She looked up. "You're in my light."

He stepped back. "I'm sorry." There was a long pause while he watched her read, her lips moving slowly. Finally he blurted it out. "Granny doesn't give a damn about you."

She looked up again, squinting at him. "What?"

"I said Granny doesn't give a damn about you. So there's no reason for you to go out with him any more."

"I already told you once. Mind your own business."

"Don't you care what people think about you?"

"I care about me. And right now I'm trying to read."

"Well, I'm trying to do you a favor."

"Just leave me alone."

"O.K.," he said. "That's not hard." He turned and began walking away. At the end of the dock he stopped and yelled to her, "I was just trying to do you a favor, that's all." Then he ran back across the sand to the canoe. Picking up the brush, he started painting with long, wild swipes of his arm.

He was not aware that she was approaching until he heard her beach bag hit the sand a few feet away from him. He stood.

"No," Tillie said. "Go on with your painting. I just thought you might like some company." She lay down beside him, her head resting on her arm.

"I'm sorry, Peter," she whispered. "I didn't mean that out there. I guess I'm not awake yet."

"Forget it. It was my fault."

"Anyway, I'm sorry."

He nodded and went on painting. "I want to go out with you tonight."

"Can't. I'm busy."

"With Granny?"

"Maybe."

"Tomorrow night, then."

"Nope."

"Why not?"

"I just don't want to go out with you, that's all."

"You went out with me yesterday. I bought you cookies, for chrissakes."

"That was lunch. I mean out."

"Why won't you?"

"That's my business."

"O.K.," he muttered. "You do what you please. I certainly don't care. One way or the other. It's no skin off my nose."

"Good."

"How about lunch today?" he said quickly. "Will you go in town with me again? Will you?"

"Sure."

He paused. "Well, maybe I don't feel like taking you."

"Suit yourself."

He turned to her. "That's not the truth," he began. "I do want to take you. I wanted to see you today. I got down here hours ago. I thought you'd be here. Where were you? What took you so long?"

"Well, first of all I overslept. And then I spent a half hour going through my word book. Then I did my exercises. Then I had to go up and say good morning to Aunt Gert. Then . . ."

"I thought you shared a cabin with her down here."

Tillie nodded. "I do. But right now she's living at The Lodge. She's got a lot of work. She'll be moving down when camp starts. In a month. Boy, she was really busy this morning. That new counselor came in."

"What new counselor?" Peter asked. "Who?"

"Chad Kimberley," Tillie said.

"What's wrong?"

Peter stopped painting and sat down. "Chad Kimberley. Is he here? Did you see him?"

"Sure, I saw him."

"How about that," Peter said. "Chad Kimberley's here."

"Is he a friend of yours?"

"No. Not really. Not to speak to or anything like that. But I know all about him, of course. He's from my home town. Everybody back there knows all about him. He scored five touchdowns against Wesleyan. Just last fall. He made all-East but he should have made all-American. Anyway, I think so. He went to the same high school I did. Everybody there still talks about him. He was valedictorian of his class. He's just a great guy, that's all."

"Anyway," Tillie said. "He's here."

"Goddam," Peter said. "What do you think of that?" He picked up the paintbrush, then set it down again. "Are you sure it was Chad Kimberley?"

"Of course I'm sure. I met him. Tall, blond. Sort of thin. Very good looking."

"That sounds like him all right," Peter nodded.

"How about that. I didn't know he was going to be up here."

"Jesus," Tillie muttered. "Let's change the subject."

"O.K.," Peter said. "O.K." He sat quietly for a moment, then reached for the paintbrush. "What do you want to talk about?"

"I don't know."

"Did you happen to see the morning paper? Do you remember how the White Sox did?"

"What are they?"

"Are you kidding? Don't you like sports?"

"No."

"Well, I do. I'm a terrific sports fan. I've got an autographed baseball from Joe DiMaggio."

"From who?"

"Joe DiMaggio. God, don't you know anything? Joe DiMaggio."

"Sounds like a wop."

"He's not. He's a baseball player. He's the greatest center fielder that ever lived. My father took me down to see him play in Comiskey Park when I was little. He hit a home run. He beat the White Sox all by himself. And I've got his autograph."

"What does it say?"

"It says, 'To Peter. Good luck from Joe Di-Maggio.'"

"Big deal."

"You're damn right it's a big deal," Peter said, his voice growing louder. "He autographed it for me." He pointed toward the dock. "Why don't you go back out there and get brown."

"What is it with everybody today?" Tillie began. "Everybody's acting like . . . like God knows what. Who cares if you got a baseball from some wop?

My old man once shook hands with Jean Harlow and it didn't make him king of the mountain."

"No kidding," Peter said. "That's great."

"What's so great about it?"

"I don't know." He thought a moment, then shrugged. "It just is."

"Yeah? Well, it didn't stop him from kicking off a couple months later. So where's the big deal?"

He did not reply. They lapsed into silence. The sun burned down; they both began to perspire. Tillie stood and walked back to the dock and began to swim. Peter went on painting. When he had slapped the last touches of green on the canoe, he called to her. She nodded, dried herself, and together they set off toward town.

Throughout that afternoon, Peter Bell had the strange but distinct feeling of time repeating itself. They lunched again at the drugstore in Cherokee. As they left the old man did not confront them, preferring instead to remain seated on the sidewalk bench, staring at Tillie as she walked past. But that was the only change. For again they sat talking on the dock, and again he delighted in watching her, close behind him, beautiful, her face and body golden from her hours in the sun.

Then, as the afternoon faded, as it began growing dark, Peter tensed, staring down the dusty road, waiting for Granny to appear. Probably she grew nervous too, but he did not think to notice; he was too busy concentrating on the road, awaiting the arrival of the red convertible.

The sun lingered one final moment, then fell. They waited, not talking now but just sitting quietly side by side. Finally two headlights flashed at the far end of the road and he heard the car's motor gunning. The headlights grew stronger, brighter, approaching through the summer dusk.

"It's Granny," Peter said.

"I know. He's late."

"You better get started."

"I will."

"I mean, you wouldn't want to keep him waiting," he went on.

She stood and, as she had done the day before, she brushed her slender hands across her skirt. She started walking away.

"Don't go," Peter said then.

"Maybe I'll see you tomorrow," Tillie muttered.

"Don't go," he repeated. "Please."

"I got to," she whispered. Then she turned and ran down the dock. He watched as she opened the front door, watched as the car jammed into reverse, watched as they drove back along the dusty road. He watched until they were gone.

Then, more from memory than desire, he rose and sprawled across the low diving board. Leaning down, he trailed his right hand in the water, looking at the lights reflecting from the houses on the far side of the lake.

The sound of footsteps made him sit up and he stared through the darkness. Someone was walking toward him. He waited, trembling. The figure stopped. Peter stood. The figure took another step. Peter did not move, but peered instead, squinting at the undiscernible outline in front of him.

"Who's there?" he said sharply.

Chad Kimberley moved out of the shadows. . . .

vii

It was on an October afternoon that Peter Bell first became fully conscious of the existence of Chad Kimberley. A Saturday afternoon, warm, still wet from a morning rain. He had ridden his bicycle up to the high school athletic field to watch the football game. He was in the seventh grade at the time, and he bought a program and picked his way through the crowded grandstand until he found a place in the corner of the topmost row and there he sat, blowing into his cupped hands, knees together, huddled, waiting for the game to begin. The field was soggy and he stared, completely detached, watching as the two teams clawed slowly at each other, moving up and down the field like multi-colored centipedes.

Then, in the second quarter, a single figure burst free and ran the length of the field, and the quiet grandstand came alive; the cheerleaders jumped and their short skirts swirled around and around, and the roaring seemed to linger, caught in the thick October air. Peter had glanced at his program and seen the name Kimberley, and a sudden stream of half-hidden images flowed disconnectedly behind his eyes, and he remembered a bronzed boy lounging by the country club pool, regally surrounded, always surrounded by a flock of others, stunting, playing, trying to please.

The Kimberleys, along with the Kempers, the Farmers, and Jacob Bell, made up the financial elite at the country club. But Jacob Bell had never associated much with the Kimberleys; Mrs. Kimberley collected Dufys; Mr. Kimberley played tennis; Jacob Bell did neither, but they would always nod to one another whenever they met, cordially, distinctly, in financial recognition.

When he reached high school, Peter found that Chad was still remembered, and as his four years fell away the memory grew until the name was not mentioned casually, but with a kind of awe. Chad had gone East to college, had done well, and Peter followed his career religiously, reading about him in the football articles of the Sunday *Tribune*. Occasionally, during college vacations, Chad would revisit the high school and Peter would follow him, staring, standing in the corners of the linoleum-lined corridors, watching the tall blond boy and the crowd of young men and women who always surrounded him, who always moved when he moved, laughed when he laughed, an additional appendage.

Probably an outsider would have termed it a common case of hero worship. But Peter Bell thought it was more. For he knew, as he had known since that October afternoon, that had he ever been given the opportunity of changing lives with Chad Kimberley, of swapping souls and bodies and minds; had he ever been given that glorious chance, he unhesitatingly would have taken it. . . .

They stared at one another for a moment. Then the taller boy spoke. "You're Peter Bell, aren't you?"

Peter nodded.

"I'm Chad Kimberley."

"Yes. I know."

They stood quietly on the dock. Peter waited, his hands clasped behind him. His mouth felt very dry. "I was watching you from back on the beach," Chad began. "I didn't want to interrupt. Then when she left . . ."

"You wouldn't have been interrupting anything."

"She's very beautiful."

"Yes. She is."

"Is she a friend of yours?"

"I hope so. I like her very much."

Chad nodded. "She spends the days with you and the nights with Granny. Is that it?"

"So far. But he doesn't even care about her. I told her that already. I don't know why she goes out with him. All he probably does is spend the time looking at himself. I never saw anybody like that before. Stare at himself the way he does."

Chad laughed. "You're right. Granny's so narcissistic he doesn't need a mirror."

"That's it!" Peter said excitedly, his voice suddenly loud. "That's exactly it."

"How do you mean?"

"Well, I saw him lifting weights. He was going at it like crazy. And I mean that. Just like he was crazy. And I knew then there was something funny but I couldn't figure it out. But that's what it was. He didn't have a mirror."

"When was this, Peter?"

"Yesterday. Yesterday in the morning."

Chad laughed again. "He must have just found out I was coming up for the summer. I called yesterday morning. Granny was getting rid of tension. He always does that."

"Why should your coming up here upset him?"

"Didn't you know?" Chad said. "I'm surprised he hasn't told you. Granny hates me."

"Why?"

"We had a falling out. Let's put it that way."

"Over what?"

"You like asking questions, don't you, Peter?"

"Yes. I'm sorry. I'm always doing that."

Chad nodded and walked to the end of the dock, staring out at the moonlight. Peter turned and followed him, stopping a few paces behind. "It's so beautiful up here," Chad said. "I always forget. It surprises me every year. It never fails to surprise me."

"It's very lovely," Peter answered, and they were quiet again.

"Are you watching me now, Peter?" Chad said softly, not turning. "Are your eyes on me?"

"Yes," Peter muttered.

"You always used to watch me at the country club. Didn't you, Peter? By the pool?"

"Yes."

"And sometimes when I came back to high school. You watched me then too."

"Yes."

"Why, Peter?" Chad turned quickly, facing the younger boy. "Why?"

"I don't know. I suppose I was trying to copy you. I saw you make a run in high school. Everybody cheered. I guess I wanted to be like you. That was why."

"Are you always so honest, Peter?"

"I never lie. Almost never, anyway. I used to when I was little. I wasn't much good at it."

"Are you still trying to copy me?"

"Yes. I guess I am."

Chad smiled. "I'll tell you what," he said. "Why don't we go have some supper? Just you and I."

"I'd like that."

"Fine. And then, afterward, we can talk. Unless you have something else planned."

"No. I haven't."

"I know a fine place for talking," Chad began. "It's . . ."

"Yes," Peter interrupted. "I found it last night. You cut your initials in the tree stump."

"Shall we go then?"

"Yes," Peter said. "I'd like that. Let's go. . . ."

"I found this spot eight years ago," Chad was saying. They were sitting close together in the clearing, staring out at the water. It was late in the evening, and the stars had begun to fade. "The first year of camp. I always thought of it afterward as belonging to me. So I never told anyone about it."

"I didn't know you were here then," Peter said.

Chad nodded. "My father gave Jeff half the money for camp. He never talked much about it. I don't know why. Probably because he's like that. Granny's dad gave the other half. It was pure snobbery. Just so their children could have some uncontaminated place to spend the summers. Jeff was

50

our gym teacher in grammar school. He did a lot for us."

"And you've been here every year?"

"That's right."

"Then why was Granny surprised to find out you were coming?"

Chad was silent for a moment. "Because he didn't expect me. Not this summer."

"Why didn't he?"

Chad smiled. "What are you going to be after college, Peter? An interrogator?"

"No."

"What, then?"

"I'm going to be a writer. I've already got an idea for a book. When I'm old enough I'm going to write it."

"Do you want to tell me what it's about?"

"Oh, I don't mind telling you. It's about everything. The whole world. I'm going to put it all in. Every thing, every place, everybody. That's probably why I ask so many questions. There's so much I want to know."

"Am I going to be in it, Peter? Are you going to put me in it?"

"Yes."

"And Granny? And the girl?"

"Yes. I told you. I'm going to put everything in. The whole shooting match. All of it."

Chad stood and walked to the edge of the clearing. He looked down at the water. "Perhaps we might talk about it tomorrow," he said, raising his eyes to the fading stars. "We'll work together. Down at the waterfront. You and I, Peter. Would you like that?"

"Yes."

Chad turned and faced him. "Come here, Peter."

Peter got up and walked over. "Here I am."

"Do you like me, Peter?"

"Yes."

"Very much?"

"Yes."

"Then will you do what I do? Will you go where I go? Will you see what I see?"

"If I can."

"Will you try?"

"Yes."

Chad's arms went around him, held him tight. He stood still, not resisting, waiting for the arms to grow loose. Chad stepped away then, turning his face to the wind.

"What is it?" Peter said finally. "What's wrong?"

"Nothing," Chad whispered, his face still averted, his blond hair soft in the moonlight. "Nothing. Not any more. Everything's fine now. . . ."

Peter Bell awoke the next morning and looked out through the screen window. Dew still clung to the wet grass, but as the sun rose higher it began to disappear, so that the ground was covered with a faint, green mist. He sat on the edge of the bed and stretched, yawning. Then, he slipped into his wooden bathing clogs and headed for the latrine.

He shaved slowly, and then he showered, letting the water sting him into consciousness. Finished, he tucked his towel around his waist and walked back to cabin number six, listening to the clicking of his wooden clogs on the cement. When he opened the cabin door, he stopped. Granny was sitting on the bed, wearing his blue shorts, smoking.

Peter nodded and began getting dressed.

Granny spoke first. "You getting used to things around here?"

"Yes. No thanks to you."

Granny took a deep inhale, holding the smoke in his lungs, then blowing it out sharply through his nostrils. "I've been busy," he said. "I haven't had a chance to give you much personal attention."

"That's fine," Peter said.

"Things will be easing up now. Some more guys are due up this afternoon."

Peter brushed his hair quickly and went to the door. "I'm going for some breakfast," he said.

"Hold on, buddy boy."

Peter stopped. "What is it?"

"I haven't told you what you're going to do today."

"I'm working at the waterfront."

"No." Granny shook his head. "No, you're not."

"Yes, I am. Chad said so. He and I are working on the waterfront today."

Granny stood. "No. You're working with me."

"I'm sorry," Peter said. "But Chad's got as much say up here as you do. And he told me I could work with him. So if you're finished, I want to go get some breakfast."

"You better stay away from Kimberley," Granny said. "You better mind what I'm telling you and stay away from him."

Peter walked out of the cabin, letting the screen door slam, and started for The Lodge. He was half-way there when Granny grabbed him and spun him around, digging his fingers into Peter's shoulders.

"Didn't you hear me? I said stay away from him."

"Let go," Peter said, trying to shake loose.

Granny shoved him backward. "Sure, buddy boy. I'll let go. But maybe there's a few things you don't know. Maybe there's a few things I could tell you about Kimberley. You don't know about him, do you, buddy boy? You don't know what happened to him."

"No," Peter said. "What?"

"He cracked up at school this year!" Granny shouted. "He cracked wide open. I thought everybody knew about Chad. He's nuts, buddy boy! Chad's nuts! He's crazy. . . ."

viii

"GRANNY SAID THAT?" Chad mused. "He still thinks that?"

"Yes," Peter nodded. "What did he mean?"

They were walking slowly across the baseball diamond, away from the center of camp.

"Granny never understood, I suppose. I told you last night. He hates me."

"Why?"

Chad shrugged. "I don't know why. Not exactly. But probably because he thinks I betrayed him, failed him, left him. He used to love me, you know. In his own way. He used to be my shadow. Until this year."

The baseball diamond lay behind them as they

continued, Chad a half step in front, walking toward the council ring; a small, open-air structure, circular, with rows of wooden benches bounded by a low birch railing. In the center lay a round fireplace, lined with rocks. At the open end of the ring stood a large wooden cross, eight feet high.

"Have you ever been here before, Peter?"

"No."

"It only gets used twice a week. On Sundays. In the morning, Jeff holds services here. At night all the campers come down and sit and talk and they light the fire. It's very pretty at night. I think you'll like it here. I do."

"What's the cross for?"

"The cross?" Chad smiled. "Mostly a joke. Jeff isn't very religious. He had it put in the first year of camp. He stands in front of it when he holds services. I think it makes him feel secure. It gives an air of importance to what he says." He walked over and stood in front of it. "Do you see what I mean?"

"Why did Granny say that?" Peter asked. "Is it true?"

"What do you think, Peter?"

"I'd just like to know, that's all."

Chad sat down on a bench near the cross. Peter sat a few feet away, quietly watching the older boy.

"I've never told anyone. Not the whole story. Never. Not even the doctors."

"Will you tell me?"

Chad stared at the ground a moment. Then he reached down and pulled up a handful of grass, holding it, his eyes closed. Finally he opened his eyes and looked at Peter Bell. Peter waited.

"All right," Chad said softly. "I'll tell you. If you'll listen."

"I will. I promise."

Chad was quiet again, and when he did start to talk his voice was very low. "It begins like this," he said. "It was the last game of my senior year, and when I woke up in the morning . . ."

It was the last game of my senior year, and when I woke up in the morning, I knew that something was going to happen. I don't quite know how to say it. I felt odd, somehow detached, separated from myself. I felt as if I were standing above myself, staring down, watching myself as I moved. My body, my entire body seemed almost to be acting on its own initiative. My arms didn't feel as though they belonged to me, but I knew that they did, because I could see them swinging from my shoulders as I walked. My legs the same way. They followed each other down the halls of the frat house, first one, then the other, but I didn't seem to have anything to do with them. They were on their own.

All my fraternity brothers wished me luck and I thanked them, told them I could use it. But I didn't know what they were wishing me luck for. Then I remembered that it was the last game of my senior year and that I didn't care. Always in the past I'd been nervous before a game, scared to death that I might make a mistake, blow a signal, fumble, not do what everyone expected me to do. But here it was, my last game, and I didn't care.

I can't remember much of what happened between getting up and game time. I'm not even sure now who we were playing, but I think it was Wesleyan. There's so much I can't remember—I've blocked it all out. But the next thing I do remember clearly was standing on the goal line, looking out at the stadium. It was full, full of people and colors, scarves and caps and coats, and I was standing on the goal line, waiting for the kick-off. But it wasn't me that was standing on the goal line. Somebody was there, all right, but it wasn't me. I was up high again, looking down, watching it all.

Then the whistle blew and everyone started to yell and then the ball was in my arms. I stood there with the ball in my arms and everyone was running, everyone except me. I was still standing there. Then Granny was shouting to me at the top of his voice, "This way, baby. This way," and I started up behind him. I followed him for a few steps and then suddenly I cut away from him, away from my interference, away from everybody, over to the far sideline. And then I was running down that sideline all by myself, and nobody could catch me. It was like a finger snap—like that—that quick—and I was standing on the other goal line, still all by myself, the ball in my hands, and everyone in the stadium, all those colors rose up and started shouting and then Granny was hugging me and the others and I tore loose and trotted upfield, waiting for the extra point. I made that too, so it was seven-nothing and I kicked off. I ripped into the ball and it shot off my foot, shot over everyone's head, and it was their ball on the twenty.

They didn't gain, so they punted out of bounds, and it was our ball again. I was standing in back of the line, waiting for the snap from scrimmage, when suddenly I remembered I'd forgotten the play. I didn't know what it was. For the first time in my life I'd forgotten the play, but I knew right then that it didn't matter. It didn't make any difference what the play was. Because no one was going to

tackle me. No one could. I knew that. So when the
ball came I just started to run and a few of them
tried grabbing at me but they couldn't hold me. I
kicked free and kept on and they were all behind
me again, except for the safety man. He was
crouched up ahead, waiting, and I could have run
around him on either side but I didn't. I went
straight at him and he went down and I ran over
him and then I was free.

There wasn't anyone between me and the goal
line and I ducked my head and started to cry, because there wasn't anyone left in front of me. So I
stopped. Right there in the middle of the field I
stopped and fell to my knees and the play was dead.
But it didn't matter because I knew I could do it
again. And that was what I wanted. To do it again.

So on the next play I dove into the center of the
line and the same thing happened. No one could
stop me. Some of them tried. They tied grabbing
at me, reaching out for me, but they couldn't do
it, and I wanted to tell them to stop trying; I wanted
to tell them all to quit because they couldn't stop
me. Nothing could.

I scored four touchdowns in the first quarter and
then the coach took me out and I sat on the bench
crying, because there it was, just the end of the first
quarter, and I was sitting on the bench already
watching the others. I put my head in my hands
and I cried. I cried until I couldn't cry any more.
The score got worse and worse and when the half
came, we were slaughtering them. At half time all
the others mobbed me and slapped me on the back
and yelled and I just stood there, shaking my head.
I didn't know why they were doing it. I wanted to
tell them that it was only because nobody could
stop me; it wasn't hard to do if you knew that no-

body could stop you. But I didn't say a word. Not to any of them.

And then it was the third quarter and they scored a couple with our scrubs in and I was watching it all from the bench. And then with about two minutes left to play in the game we had the ball deep in our own territory and the coach sent me in again. The next thing the ball was in my arms and I knew what was going to happen. I didn't even want it to happen. I didn't want to run any more and I tried not to but my legs wouldn't stop and my arms wouldn't stop and everybody else was slipping and falling down in the grass. I couldn't help it. I ran the length of the field trying to stop or trip or fall or something but I couldn't help it. My legs kept on going and then I'd scored again and I started running back to the bench.

But they wouldn't let me. The crowd wouldn't let me. They were all standing up and waving banners and the colors made patterns and they screamed my name, "KIMBERLEY! KIMBERLEY! KIMBERLEY!" louder and louder and I stopped at midfield and let it wash over me. It swelled until I thought my eardrums would split with the sound, my name, my name, always my name. It was all I could hear, just that, my own name, and I wanted to cry harder than I ever wanted to cry before, but I couldn't. I couldn't cry and I couldn't move so I started yelling with them. "KIMBERLEY!" I yelled. "KIMBERLEY!" until the coach came out and led me off the field. He led me through the tunnel to the locker room with me still yelling my own name, and all the way through the tunnel I could feel the walls shake from the stamping up above.

The locker room was jammed. With old grads

and reporters from New York, all of them asking me questions. They asked me the same questions, over and over again, and I answered them, and that went on for I don't know how long before they let me go.

It was the same back at the frat house. Jammed. Worse than the locker room, and I tried to sneak in but they caught sight of me and grabbed me and lifted me up on their shoulders, carrying me from one room to the next. They were yelling and the noise was terrible and they were reaching up to touch me and then somebody handed me a drink and I drank it while I was being carried around, in and out of rooms, my feet never once on the floor. They were all reaching up to touch me, girls, boys, all of them reaching up to touch me, laughing and still yelling my name out loud.

After a while I scrambled down and tried leaving, because I had a date in New York and I told them I had to get moving or I'd be late. But they wouldn't let me go. They kept pulling at me and dragging me back until finally I had to tear loose from them. I ran to the parking lot and jumped into my convertible and drove off.

Her first name was Prisilla. I can't remember her last name. But she was eighteen years old and she was pretty and virginal and rich. Big rich. Her father had owned something, I can't remember what. A chain of stores; something. He was getting a divorce when he died and he left everything to Prisilla, not a cent to her mother.

I met her at nine o'clock in the Oak Room at the Plaza. That was one of the only places she was allowed to go. She wasn't allowed to go on week ends or to just any restaurant. Her mother had a list, and Prisilla had to stick to it. And the funny thing about that was that her mother was a lush. Not a penny to her name and an alcoholic, but she still watched over her girl like a great mother hen.

I was sitting at a table in the corner when she came in. She was wearing a black cocktail dress with just a single strand of pearls and pearl earrings. Very simple and plain. She always dressed that way. Simple and plain. It suited her. God, she was pretty. Really a pretty little girl. But so stupid. And so cold. I wanted her just because she was so cold. It was like a game we played. I kept taking her out because I wanted her and she wouldn't let me; she was the only one I can think of that wouldn't let me. Anyway, she walked over and sat down and asked me how the game was.

And I couldn't remember. I didn't know. I wasn't sure. Then suddenly I started to shake and I yelled for a waiter and everyone looked at me but I didn't care. I had to find out so I gave the waiter ten dollars and told him to get me a newspaper and to hurry because I had to know. I sat there waiting for him to come back. I sat there waiting and he didn't come and he didn't come and then finally he did and I told him to keep the change. Then I started to open the paper.

But I couldn't do it. I just sat there with that pretty little girl beside me, holding the paper in my hands, holding it as tight as I could. Finally I shoved the paper at Prisilla and told her to open it and she did and I asked what it said and she began to laugh.

I looked at the headline. "Kimberley Scores Five!" It was right there, black and white, and I started laughing too, because now I knew I hadn't made it up, that it had really happened. I read the article over and over, just to make certain, and Prisilla wouldn't believe I hadn't known. She kept trying to make jokes about it and when I didn't listen she began running her fingers up and down my arm, pushing her body against mine, whispering to me, touching me with her hands. Then a couple of men came over from the bar and asked, "Aren't you Chad Kimberley?" and I said I was and they bought us a few drinks. And then a bigger crowd started to gather around our table and somebody with a camera tried to take my picture and I drank and drank but it didn't affect me. I wanted to get drunk but I couldn't. I just sat there and said, "Yes, I'm Chad Kimberley. Yes, I'm Chad Kimberley," until finally we left.

It was late in the evening by that time. Prisilla lived on Fifth Avenue in the Seventies, and we took a hansom cab through Central Park, then out of it again, up to her building. She and her mother shared the penthouse, but when we got there her mother was out. We walked onto the terrace and she put her arms around me and I knew right then that I could have her if I wanted her. And I did want her. Except that I knew I was waiting for something. So I waited, her with her arms still around me, holding me tight, her body shaking. From the terrace you could see Central Park South with all the neon signs flashing from the tops of the buildings, giving the time, the weather, flashing on and off and I stood there, watching the minutes change.

Finally we went into the living room and sprawled down on a long, dark green sofa. It was soft; soft as a feather bed and we lay there. I was still waiting while Prisilla kept running her hands over my body, holding me tighter than before. She was looking up at me, scared to death and it showed in her eyes and I knew I could have her. I knew that at last I could have her and that she wanted me to have her, but I was still waiting. I waited and waited and then it happened.

Her mother came in. Blind drunk. She rolled into the room, looking at us in the darkness. There weren't any lights on in the room but the moonlight came through the terrace windows and I watched her. She was hardly able to walk but she tried anyway, moving from one piece of furniture to the next, grabbing at them for support. She kept saying "good evening, good evening," and "did we have a nice time," but she gave that up after a while and collapsed into the green chair across from the sofa. She sat there, no more than six feet away from us, talking again, talking, mumbling about I don't know what.

Then she passed out. Without a word of warning. She passed out cold, six feet away from us, her head up, her eyes still half open.

I started fumbling with Prisilla's dress and she whispered "no, no, no, no," but she didn't stop me, didn't really try. Every so often she glanced over at her mother who stared back at her with those dead half-open eyes. She was scared more than before, at least at the start. She was afraid that her mother was going to wake up and see us, but I wasn't. Because she couldn't wake up. She couldn't and I knew it. She was what I'd been waiting for and she wasn't about to wake up now and spoil everything. Prisilla caught on finally and we lay there on that dark green sofa, with me on top of her, both of us trying to quiet our breathing as best we could. And then I felt myself leaving myself again, rising up above, staring down; me watching me doing what I was doing, saying, "Yes, Chad, go on, Chad, you're right, Chad, go on, Chad, go on."

Prisilla was crying when I stood up to leave. I walked across to the green chair and closed her mother's eyes. Then I went to the door and said good night and left.

I started down Fifth Avenue but after a few blocks I cut into Central Park in the direction of the Plaza. I walked slowly at first but then I began to hurry, picking up the step, almost running, and I didn't know why. All I did know was that I had to get back to the Plaza.

And the next thing I heard was my own voice and it was shouting, "I'm Chad Kimberley. I'm Chad Kimberley," as loud as it could. I started to run because then I knew why I had to get back to the Plaza. I fell a few times, it was so dark, but I jumped up again and went on, cutting through the park. I had to get back to the Plaza because that was where I'd left the newspaper and I had to have that newspaper, I just had to. So I ran and my voice was shouting my name and then I tripped and fell down hard and lay still.

Someone was following me.

From off in the distance I could hear someone running and I knew he was trying to catch me so I got up and started running again but I couldn't seem to go fast enough, because the footsteps kept getting louder and louder and the ground began to shake.

I turned around and waited.

I can't remember much of what he looked like. I think he was dressed in rags and I think he was a cripple, but I'm not sure. All I do remember are his eyes. He had the biggest eyes I've ever seen. But they had no color. They were almost transparent; I could almost see through them. He stared at me. I couldn't move. He came closer, staring at me with those eyes and I couldn't move. Then he brought his face up close to mine and his eyes grew even bigger. His face was next to mine, an inch away, and I remember that he had no breath. I couldn't feel his breath on my face even though he was right next to me, only an inch away.

"What do you want?" I said. "What do you want from me?"

"Help," he said.

"Yes," I said. "Anything."

"You've got to help me."

"Yes," I said again. "Just tell me what you want me to do." I waited, and finally he said it.

"Nobody knows I'm alive," he said. "So you've got to help me. Nobody knows I'm alive. So you've got to think about me. Because if you think about me then someone will know and I'll be alive. So you've got to think about me because nobody knows I'm alive."

Then he was gone.

I waited. He didn't come back. I took a step, then stopped. "I'm thinking about you," I said. I started to run and every step I took I thought about him. I didn't stop thinking about him once, all the way back to the Plaza.

But when I got there I didn't know why I'd come. I couldn't remember. There was something about a newspaper but that didn't make any sense. I said, "I'm thinking about you," out loud and one of the doormen asked was there something but I shook my head and jumped into a taxi and took it back to where I'd parked my car and all the time I was in the taxi I said, "I'm thinking about you," until the driver asked me what I was saying so I stopped saying it out loud. But I thought it to myself, "I'm thinking about you, I'm thinking about you," over and over until I got back to the garage.

Somehow I made it out of New York and through the tunnel and then I was on the highway, hitting a hundred miles an hour. The top was down and the wind tore by and I could scream it again, out loud, "I'M THINKING ABOUT YOU! I'M THINKING ABOUT YOU! I'M THINKING ABOUT YOU!" and after my voice gave out I kept on screaming it, even though there wasn't any sound.

When I reached the frat house I ran inside and woke everybody up and told them to come into my room. And when they were all there I told them about the man and how we all had to think about him so someone would know he was alive.

And they laughed. They were the same ones who had carried me around on their shoulders just a few hours before; they were the same ones who had reached up just to touch me a few hours before. And now they were laughing at me. I tried to quiet them, tried to tell them there wasn't anything funny, that I meant it. But they wouldn't listen to me. They laughed and swore and then they left me, most of them, they left me to do it all by myself.

I tried explaining it to Granny, but he wouldn't understand. I went around to the rooms again and tried explaining it to them, but they wouldn't understand. I never stopped thinking about him though; not once all that time.

Then a bunch of them grabbed me and tried putting me to bed and I let them. I didn't struggle. But when they were gone I left the dorm in my pajamas and went out by myself to a wood on the edge of the college and I sat down against a tree and watched the sun rise. I stared at the sun and I thought about him and when the sun was out of sight, over my head, I stared at the sky and I thought about him, and when the sky grew dark I watched it and I thought about him.

Granny found me.

They were all out looking but it was Granny who found me. He stood in front of me and told me to get up. I didn't move. He knelt down in front of me and told me to get up but I still didn't move. He looked so funny. It was as though I was watching him through the big end of a giant telescope, and he looked so funny, so small, that I had to laugh. He told me to stop laughing and I could hardly hear him, he was so small. But somehow I knew what he was saying and he looked so funny kneeling down there that I laughed again and again. Then he started screaming, shaking me, screaming at me to stop laughing but I couldn't, he looked so funny. Then he started to hit me. His knees wide apart he swung at me, hitting me over and over, but I couldn't feel anything, he was so small. He smashed at my face with his fists and I sat there laughing at him while he screamed at me and swung out at my face and I suppose he never would have stopped if some of the others hadn't heard him and found us and pulled him away, still screaming.

Then they lifted me and carried me back. . . .

"What happened next?" Peter said. He was sitting cross-legged on the ground, watching as Chad paced around the council ring.

"Oh, not much. The rest is all kind of anticlimactic. That happened a little more than six months ago. They sent me home. The school did, and I

68

stayed home for a few days. It was all hushed up, of course. Then my parents sent me to a place up in Vermont."

"A sanitarium?"

Chad nodded. "Something like that. I've been there ever since. Until three days ago. They decided the summer up here might do me some good, and I didn't mind. I like it here. I'll go back when the summer is over."

Peter sat quietly, his chin resting in his cupped hands.

"So now you know," Chad said. "What do you think?"

Peter shook his head. "I don't understand it. But I'm glad you told me."

"Do you think I'm crazy, Peter? Do you think Granny was right?"

"Of course not."

"Well then, what do you think?"

Peter stood. "I think it's about time we got down to the waterfront," he said, and together they set off toward the lake. . . .

On midafternoon of that same day the four of them met, Peter and Chad walking up from the beach, Granny and the girl walking down. They stopped for a moment on the cement walk. Even though he was but a few feet away from her, Peter waved.

"Hi," he said.

"Hi," Tillie nodded.

The others said nothing. Then they separated, continuing on.

That was the only time the four of them ever were together, a brief ten seconds on a cloudy afternoon. And those were the only words exchanged. "Hi," and then, "Hi."

And it seems to me now, looking back on that meeting, that there should have been more; more than just the wave, the nod, the two spoken syllables. I think perhaps that there should have been music underscoring it all; kettle drums thumping, saxophones blaring, french horns playing in rhythm a half note apart. Something. I think we deserved it. Or, at the very least, I think Chad did. . . .

ix

Of course, Peter Bell did not think that then. If he
thought about anything at all during the three days
that followed the talk in the council ring, he could
not remember later what it was. For he spent all of
his time with Chad Kimberley, and that was enough.
They worked together during the days, talked together in the evenings; Chad, bronzed and tall,
Peter, shorter, darker; always together.

But had he taken the time to think during those
three days, he would not have been at a loss for
subjects. Other counselors arrived, half a dozen of
them, one from Memphis, two from Cincinnati, the
rest from smaller scattered communities around the
Middle West. He never got to know any of them,

never really talked with any of them, other than the perfunctory introduction, the passing "hello" thereafter. They did not come near him, or near Chad, as was more probably the truth. They stayed close to Granny, and at mealtime there was always whispered laughter echoing distantly through the kitchen of The Lodge. Chad did not seem to mind; he met the laughter with a stare, fixating until it died, until quiet ranged again over the table. And Peter didn't mind either. He was too busy being with Chad, following him, watching him, copying, walking half a step behind.

He was so busy that he didn't even talk with Tillie Keck, although he managed to find out what she was doing. The boy from Memphis took her out one night, a boy from Cincinnati on another. He hated them for it, of course, but he kept his anger quiet, contained, hating at his leisure, in the mornings as he stretched and rolled around in bed, at night as he lay silently, waiting for sleep. So the three days passed; quick days in which he smiled and sang and laughed and acted like some great, large-footed puppy who had just discovered sunshine.

And then, on Saturday, as they were sitting down to lunch in the kitchen of The Lodge, he and Chad at one end of the table, the others bunched together, apart, Granny spoke to him.

"What's this about you and Tillie?" he said.

Peter flushed. "Nothing. What do you mean?"

"I was just talking to her. She told me she was going out with you tonight."

"No," Peter said. "You must have misunderstood. She doesn't want to go out with me."

Granny shrugged. "She just told me different."

"Are you sure?" Peter asked. "Are you positive?"

"Maybe not."

"Where is she? Where did you see her?"

"On the dock."

Peter jumped up from the table and hurried outside. It was a hot day and, as he raced down the cement walk to the water, perspiration poured from his face, soaked his T-shirt. At the bottom of the hill he stopped and breathed deeply several times. Then he thrust his hands into his pockets and ambled slowly out onto the dock.

Tillie Keck lay on her back, facing the sun, her etiquette book open beside her. Her skin was darker, a richer gold. She wore a different white bathing suit, and a faint moist film covered her face and body. Occasionally she licked out with her tongue, back and forth between her lips, wetting them. Peter shouted to her and she sat quickly, bracing her body with her elbows, waiting.

"Hey," he began. "Hey. Granny just told me that you told him that we were going out tonight. Together. Did you say that?"

"Maybe."

"Are you going to go out with me, Tillie? Do you want to? Do you really want to?"

"Do you?"

"Oh yes," Peter said. "I'd like that."

"O.K., then," Tillie nodded.

"You mean it's set? For tonight?"

"Sure."

"Just the two of us, I mean. I'll be alone and you won't bring anybody either. O.K.?"

"What are you talking about?"

"Well, I just wanted to know for sure what you meant. I like to have everything straight. So there won't be any mix-up or anything like that. I don't go out with girls much." He turned and started back toward the beach.

"Hey," she shouted after him. "What time?"

"Time," he said, stopping. "I forgot that." He paused. "How about after supper. Is that all right?"

"O.K.," and she lay flat again.

He took a few more steps, then stopped. "Hey, Tillie," he called. "Shouldn't I know where to pick you up? I mean, where do you want to meet?"

"My place," and she pointed. "The third cabin down."

He stared along the row of summer cottages that led toward the town. "The white one?"

"Yes," she shouted.

"O.K., then," he yelled. "It's all set. Just the two of us. After supper. At your place. The third one down. Everything's straight." He began running across the beach. Then he stopped and turned one final time. "Thank you, Tillie," he shouted. "Thank you." Then he hurried up the hill.

Lunch was over when he got to The Lodge. Gert was filing papers in the office.

"Hi," Peter said, walking in. "Do you know what? I'm going out with Tillie tonight." Gert nodded. "I thought maybe you could tell me what she likes to do. I don't go out with girls much and I wouldn't want to do anything that she wouldn't like."

"I can't help you," Gert said, her back to him. "What she does is none of my affair."

"But you're her aunt. You must know something."

"What she does is none of my affair," Gert repeated. She sat down and wiped her forehead. "And right now I'm very busy. I've got a lot to do. Jeff's coming back and I've got to have everything in order."

"When is he coming?"

"Late tonight. Or early tomorrow. One or the other."

"You sure there's nothing you can tell me? Any hints or anything?"

"What she does...." Gert began.

"I know," Peter interrupted. "None of your affair."

He walked into the kitchen and made himself two sandwiches and poured himself a large glass of milk. Eating quickly, he rinsed the glass and hurried back across the lawn to cabin number six.

Chad was waiting for him.

"Hi," Peter said, letting the door slam shut behind him. "Guess what? I've got a date tonight. With Tillie. Isn't that something?"

Chad did not answer.

"What do you think I ought to do with her?" Peter went on. "What do you think she'd like? I don't go out with girls much so I don't really know. What do you think? Tell me."

"I don't want you to go out with her," Chad said.

"Well, I am. But I don't exactly know what to do with her. There's just going to be the two of us, though. She's not bringing anybody and neither am I. Isn't that great? And all the time I thought she didn't want to have a date with me."

"Don't go," Chad said. He sat up on the edge of the bed and stared at Peter Bell.

"For Chrissakes why not? What are you saying that for?"

"I'm asking you not to go. That ought to be enough."

"Well, it isn't, Chad. Come on, now. What are you talking about?"

Chad stood and walked to the door. "Peter," he whispered. "I'm asking you not to go. Now, what are you going to do?"

"I told her already it was set. You just can't go around breaking a date like that for no good reason. I just wish I knew what I was going to do with her, though. There really isn't much you can do around here."

"All right, Peter." He opened the door.

"Hey, wait a minute, Chad. Don't go. You've got to tell me what to do with her. You've got to help me."

"I just tried," Chad said, and he closed the door.

"Well, that's a helluva thing to say," Peter called. "Hey, Chad. Come on back here. Come on. Please."

But Chad did not stop and when he was gone, out of sight, Peter looked at himself in his hand mirror, sat down on the bed, tucked his arms into his sides, and began to shiver....

He spent the afternoon getting ready. For more than an hour he lay on his bed, thinking what to do, finally giving up. Then he tried selecting his clothes. Nothing appealed to him so he gave up again and went to shave. He shaved twice, nicking his lip, scraping the skin on his neck until it stung. Then he showered, scrubbing himself, digging at the dirt around his fingernails. Finished, he returned to his cabin and looked at the alarm. It was only three o'clock. Lying down, he folded his arms behind his head and stared at the ceiling. At three-thirty, he dressed, putting on a clean white shirt and his only pair of pressed khakis. He ran back to the latrine and surveyed himself in the full-length mirror. His shirt was already damp with perspiration so he quickly took it off and smoothed the wrinkles with his hands, walking slowly back to the cabin to hang it up. Now it was four o'clock. The sun grew hotter. He lay in bed perspiring, sweat dripping down from his forehead, stinging his eyes. The cabin was bright and hot from the sun, so he turned his face to the wall and closed his eyes, shutting out the light as best he could. He lay that way for a long time, until his neck started itching and he thought about scratching it, but his arms suddenly felt heavy. He decided against it. It was much too hot to move, he thought; there just wasn't any point at all to moving. . . .

It was dark when he awoke. Jumping out of bed, he grabbed for the alarm clock and stared. It was after eight. Throwing his shirt across his shoulders, he bolted out the door on a dead run, stumbling, regaining his balance, buttoning his shirt as he went. Stumbling again on the walk, he managed to right himself and continue on down the hill, turning left at the beach, racing for the third cottage. When he reached it, he stopped, panting, and tucked in his shirt. Then he knocked on the door.

"I'm sorry," he called. "It's me, Tillie. Peter Bell. I'm late. Are you still there?"

"Some supper," he heard.

Tillie Keck opened the door and stepped outside. She was wearing a white peasant blouse and a white cotton skirt and white sandals. Closing the door, she turned toward him. He said nothing. She fidgeted a moment, nervously, not returning his stare.

"What's the matter?" she asked finally.

"Nothing," he answered. "You look marvelous. You really do. I don't think I've ever seen you looking any better. I mean that."

She nodded. "Where you been? What kept you?"

"I had a lot of things to do."

She looked at him. "You're all sweaty."

"Oh, this is nothing," he muttered. "It's just that I perspire easily. You should see me. Sometimes I really get soaked."

"Anyway, you're here," she said. "Let's get going."

"Yes. We better."

"What are we going to do?"

"You know?" he laughed. "That's a funny thing. But I've been doing a lot of thinking on that particular subject. We could take a drive, I suppose. Except that I don't have a car." He laughed again. "To tell you the truth, Tillie, I didn't really decide on much of anything. What would you like to do?"

"You're the boy. You're supposed to take care of things like that."

"But I don't go out with girls much," he answered quickly. "Oh, I told you that once already." He paused. "The truth is that I've never been out with a girl before. Not really. Not like this, I mean. Not alone. Of course I've been to parties and things. But there are usually lots of people at parties." They started walking along the edge of the lake, kicking at the sand. "And I've been to the country club a lot, too. Well, not a lot, really. But I've been there. I don't like it much."

"What kind of a place is it?"

"Oh, it's very nice. You know, with a pool and a golf course and tennis courts. All very spiffy. Except that I don't like it."

"Are you rich?"

"I guess so. My father is anyway. Would you like to go canoeing?"

"What?"

"I just wondered if you'd like to go canoeing." He stopped. "Would you? I'm a terrible canoeist but we could take one of those green ones I painted. What do you say?"

She shrugged. "O.K., I guess."

"I'm a terrible canoeist," he said again. "But don't you worry. I'm very careful. You just wait right here and I'll do the rest."

He sat down on the sand and took off his moccasins and ran to get a canoe. Carrying it, he waded out and dropped it into the water with a splash.

"O.K., now," he told her. "You take my shoes and I'll carry you out."

He lifted her and waded to the side of the canoe and placed her in the stern, facing the bow. Then he put one foot in the canoe, shoved as hard as he could with the other, and they glided past the end of the dock, where a current caught them and they drifted gently out toward the center of the lake. The water was very smooth and the moon felt almost warm, like the sun. Peter smiled, looking at her. She sat very straight, her hands gripping the gunwales.

"I don't know if this was such a red-hot idea," Tillie said, after a while. "I don't much feel like getting wet."

"Oh, canoes are very safe," Peter assured her. "They never tip over or anything like that. Not if you're careful."

They were quiet again. From somewhere in the distance they heard the sound of music. Peter listened a moment. "Someone's playing his victrola awfully loud," he said.

"It's from in town."

"How can you tell?"

"They're having a dance tonight. I think they

have them every Saturday." She leaned forward suddenly. "Hey! That's what let's do. Let's go dancing."

"No."

"Why not?"

"I never learned how."

"You're kidding."

Peter shook his head and watched the water for a while. Finally he looked at her. "I did go to dancing school once, though. One time. When I was little. It was terrible."

"What was so terrible about it?"

He trailed his hand in the water. "Oh, everything. It was awful. The teacher was a monster. She looked like a Wagnerian soprano."

"What are they?"

"Big fat women. Cows, almost. And this dancing teacher, she looked like that. We were all little kids at the time. Not much bigger than babies. And none of us wanted to be there. Most of them were crying. Oh, it was terrible. And this dancing teacher kept clicking castanets. She had one in each hand. And she kept clicking them over and over. I can still hear them. Click-click-click. It was her way of getting us to be quiet. Of course, if she'd just told us to be quiet once, it would have worked a whole lot better. But that wasn't her way. She was big on castanets, I guess."

"Was this at the 'Y' or something?"

"Oh, no. It was very private and expensive."

"It sure doesn't sound like it."

"Well, it was. But that isn't all. The craziest thing happened after she did get us quiet. She lined us up in two long rows, facing each other. And then she signaled to the piano player—there was this old bald piano player sitting up on a platform—and he started pounding away. And then she began moving around, clicking her castanets and walking behind us. And all the time she walked, she kept saying, 'Your turn to curtsy, my turn to bow,' and she'd gesture for us to do the same thing. So we did. Or we tried anyway. Bending over and like that, saying it again and again. 'Your turn to curtsy, my turn to bow. Your turn to curtsy, my turn to bow.' Oh, it was crazy."

"Makes sense to me."

"No. You don't get what I mean. Don't you see? We were just little kids. We didn't know what she was talking about. We didn't know who was supposed to curtsy and who was supposed to bow. We didn't even know if we were boys or girls or what, we were so little. It was as if we were all the same sex, we just didn't know. And there we were, trying . . ."

"Now *that* sounds crazy," Tillie said. "That doesn't make any sense at all."

"Anyway," Peter finished, "I only went the one time."

"I'll teach you," Tillie said. "We'll go into town and I'll teach you."

"No."

"Why? Are you embarrassed?"

"Yes. But that's not it. We just can't go into town."

"Why not?"

"I forgot the paddle," Peter said.

Tillie stared at him.

"I'm sorry," he muttered. "I told you I was a terrible canoeist. I guess I got excited. Anyway, I forgot."

"Well Jesus, what are we going to do?"

"I've been thinking about that," Peter began.

"And I've decided that we've got nothing to worry about. We'll get carried back into shore. All we have to do is sit tight until that happens." He looked at her. "I'm sorry, Tillie. I really am. I knew something would happen. Are you mad?"

"No. I'm not mad."

"Good."

He nodded and sat back, his arms draped over the sides of the canoe. The evening was still warm and it felt like rain, but the sky was clear. Moonlight glistened on the water and they glided through it, rocking gently. Tillie sat straight, staring out at the water, her face in profile, her hands half hidden in the folds of her white cotton skirt.

"You've got a terrific suntan," Peter said finally. She nodded.

"You look wonderful. You really do. White's a good color for you. Did you know that? Did you? That white was a good color for you?"

She nodded again.

"I'm sorry about the paddle," he went on. "You know I didn't do it on purpose. I just get very nervous when I'm around girls. I'm very nervous now, for instance. Can you tell?"

"Maybe. I guess so."

"You know why I'm nervous, don't you? It's because I wanted to make a good impression. I wanted to do something that you'd like. I mean, what I'm trying to say is that I like you. I do, Tillie. Did you know that?"

"Maybe."

"Well, it's the truth. I do. I like you very much. And I'm sorry that I messed it up and I'm sorry that we came out here and I'm sorry about the whole thing. And what I mean is that I'd like to try it again. I'd like to go out with you again,

Tillie, and I'll do better. I will. You'll see. I'll do whatever you want, I promise. All I want is the chance. The chance to please you. That's all. And now I'll shut up. Except that I always talk a lot when I'm nervous anyway. So what I guess I mean is that I'll try to shut up. Do you understand, Tillie? Do you understand what I'm trying to tell you?"

She looked at him for a moment. Then she nodded again. "Maybe," she said very quietly. "Maybe I do. But I think that we ought to be going in now, huh?"

"If you want," Peter answered. He glanced toward shore. "It doesn't look we're drifting in very fast."

"I don't think we're drifting in at all."

"Oh, I can fix that," Peter said. "Hold on tight," and he vaulted over the side into the water.

"Hey," Tillie yelled. "Hey, what are you doing?"

"It's O.K.," he called up to her. "The water's much warmer than you'd think. It's really very nice." He grabbed hold of the bow of the canoe and started kicking his feet, stroking with his free hand, swimming for shore.

"I feel stupid," Tillie called. "Can't I do something?"

Peter released the canoe and began treading water. "No," he said. "Please. Just stay there. Right where you are. I'd like it if you'd just sit right where you are. Will you?"

She nodded, smiling, so he grabbed hold of the bow again, kicking his feet, moving slowly across the moonlit lake. She sat, regally quiet, her body straight, her hands folded in her lap. After a few minutes he stopped and swam away from the canoe and stared up at her. She smiled back at him so he lifted one hand and waved to her before returning to the bow. Soon he began to tire, and he closed his eyes, holding to the canoe for support, getting his breath.

He had no idea how long it took him, but he was exhausted when his feet touched bottom. Shoving the canoe half onto the beach, he fell on the sand and lay still, panting.

"You all right?" Tillie asked. She stood over him, looking down, holding his moccasins in her hand.

"Oh, I'm fine," he said. "I just need a second or two to catch my breath, that's all." He rolled into a sitting position, his arms locked around his knees. "It was farther than I thought."

"It was very nice of you to do that, Peter. And I appreciate it. But I think I better get home now."

"I'll take you." He struggled to his feet. They walked in silence to the cottage, and she opened the door. "Thank you very much," Peter said then. "I had a wonderful time."

She looked at him. "You kidding?"

"No. I mean it. I did. Are you going inside now?"

She nodded. "Good night."

"Wait a second, Tillie."

She stopped.

"Aren't you going to kiss me?"

"Are you asking me?"

He moved from one foot to the other. "Well, I didn't want to take you by surprise, or anything like that. I mean, I didn't want to grab you. Especially being all wet like this. I didn't think you'd like that. But would you?"

"Here," she said. "Put on your shoes." He knelt a moment, then stood up close beside her. "Now come closer." He did. "Now put your arms around me." He put his arms around her. "Now . . ."

"You don't mind all this?" he interrupted. "Do you, Tillie? I mean, you want to, don't you?"

"Shut up," she whispered. "And close your eyes." He closed his eyes. "Now," she breathed. "Kiss me."

He opened his eyes and squinted. Then he closed his eyes again. Then he kissed her. He held her very tightly and pressed his mouth down against her mouth. Then he released her.

"Thank you," he whispered. "Thank you very much."

"You're welcome."

"I really appreciate that. And I did have a wonderful evening. And I'm . . ."

"Good night, Peter," and she smiled and closed the door.

"Good night," he yelled from outside. "Good night, Tillie."

Stuffing his hands into his pockets, he began walking up the hill, his clothes already drying in the evening warmth. He saw a pebble shining in the moonlight and he kicked at it. "God damn," he said out loud, and then he broke into a run.

The light was on in The Lodge and as he walked by he could hear voices, but he did not go in. Instead, he hurried on to Chad's cabin. It was empty. He backtracked to his own cabin, but it was empty too. Finally he turned and walked across the lawn to The Lodge.

There were half a dozen of them sitting in the living room, Granny and the others, sitting around, smoking. He started past the entrance, but Granny called to him so he stopped, hesitating a moment. Then he walked into the room.

There was the sound of distant laughter and he saw money being thrown across the room, ones and

fives and tens and the laughter grew. Granny lay
sprawled full length on the sofa while the others
threw the folded bills toward him and he reached
down to the floor and picked them up, counting.
Peter blinked as the laughter increased. The air was
thick with smoke and he turned around slowly,
looking at all their faces, the only silent person in
the laughing room.

"His clothes dried pretty fast," Granny roared.
Peter spun around. "I guess you made it to shore
safely, didn't you, buddy boy? For a while there I
figured we might have to call out the Coast Guard."

"Why were you watching me? Tell me why."

"We had to, buddy boy. We had to see how our
bets came out, didn't we? You can't blame us for
that." He laughed again, louder than before, and
the sound echoed, coming from all over, crowding
the room. It rang.

"What bets?"

"We just wanted to see if you'd score, that's all.
The rest of us have. I said you wouldn't." He held
the bills high over his head and shook them. The
laughter exploded. "I guess you didn't know about
Tillie, did you, buddy boy?" Peter bent over and
put his hands to his ears. "I guess you didn't know
Tillie was a whore. But that's what she is, buddy
boy. A regular living whore. She does it for
money. . . ."

x

PETER BELL LAY RIGID in the clearing. He lay on his stomach, his body pressing hard against the pine needle floor, his arms pressing hard against his body. He was shaking, so he pushed his face into the soft earth, his dry eyes shut tight. He felt a scream building inside him and he bit down hard on his lower lip, stifling it, listening to the dry stringy sound of his own breathing.

Finally he raised his head and stared out at the lake. Far to his left, faintly outlined in the warm moonlight, he saw the silhouette of a canoe half dragged onto the beach. He stared at it for as long as he could, and then he quickly doubled up, lying on his side, his legs digging into his chest, his arms locked around them. Raising his hands to his face, he dug his fists into his eye sockets until he felt pain. He could feel the scream again, building, building, and this time he did not try to stop it; rather he listened in an almost detached way as his cry of anger shot out into the moonlight night, racing across the lake, then rebounding, softer, more distant, no longer a scream. His entire body was knotted and he dug his knees viciously into his chest, holding his breath until his lungs ached and the cords in his neck stood taut.

He felt, more strongly than at any other moment of his life, a desire for violence; he wanted to lash out, to maim some other living thing. He wanted to kill. But he did not move; he stayed where he was, lying on his side, head down, his arms around his legs, his legs pressing painfully against his chest, fetal. He waited for the tears to come but he could not cry. His neck muscles loosened. His breath came more evenly; still in gasps but still more evenly, and he released his legs and let them fall. Rolling onto his back, he began to inhale, his legs stretched out straight. His calf muscles knotting so he half sat and pounded at them with the side of his hand. Then he lay down again, flat, his dry eyes closed, breathing the pine-scented air.

In the distance he heard the faint sound of twigs snapping. The sound grew louder but he did not move. He lay flat, pulling the air into his lungs, listening to the sound as it came closer. He opened his eyes, aware that someone was standing behind him, aware of the shadow that suddenly cut across his body. But still he did not move. Neither did the shadow. They both waited.

Then Peter spoke. "Get away," he said.

"I've come for you, Peter."

"Get away, Chad."

Chad Kimberley knelt down beside him and took his hand. "I've come for you, Peter," he said again. "Get up now."

"Please," Peter whispered. "Please."

"It's all right, Peter. Everything is all right. You must believe that."

"No. No, it isn't, Chad. He humiliated me. He humiliated me."

"I know, Peter."

"I want to kill him, Chad. I want to kill him. He humiliated me."

"I know, Peter. But you must get up now." He began pulling at Peter Bell's hand.

Peter stared vaguely at the stars, shaking his head. "You don't understand, Chad. Didn't you hear what I said? He humiliated me."

"I understand, Peter. Of course I understand. But you had to learn. And now you have. I told you not to go but you didn't listen. You had to learn."

Peter sat up quickly, wrenching his hand away. "You knew?"

"Of course."

"You knew what he was doing? You knew what he was doing and you still let him? You let him humiliate me? You let him do that?"

"It was the only way you could learn," Chad said, and he reached out again, his eyes bright.

Peter crawled back toward the edge of the clearing. "You let him do that to me. You let him. What did I have to learn! What!"

"To follow me, Peter. To do as I do. To go where I go. To see what I see. And now you have."

"What's the matter with you, Chad?" What are you talking about? Get away and tell me what you're talking about."

They stood across the clearing from one another. Chad's back was to the moon, but Peter could still see his eyes. Even though his back was to the moon, Peter could still see his eyes.

Chad took a step forward.

"I'm telling you to keep away from me," Peter said, his voice rising. "Just keep away from me, Chad."

Chad halted. "You must follow me, Peter. You must stop this now and follow me."

"Well, I'm not going to follow you. I'm not going anywhere with you. So just stay away from me. And for God's sake close your eyes."

He took a step backward, out of the clearing into the wood. Chad began walking toward him. Peter stumbled, half fell, then regained his balance.

"Stop, Chad!"

Chad stopped, smiling at him.

"All right now," Peter began, fighting to keep his voice under control. "What is it, Chad? What's the matter with you? Tell me what's the matter with you."

"Yes, Peter," Chad whispered. "I'll tell you. I've never told anyone but I'll tell you. Do you remember that man, Peter? That man I met in the park?"

"Yes."

"I know who it was. I know. And I've never told anyone but I'll tell you. Because you'll understand. It was God, Peter. It was God that came to me. God stared at me in the park."

"You don't know what you're saying, Chad. You don't mean that. You don't."

"Of course I mean it. Didn't I just tell you? You're the only one I've told. Because you're the only friend I've got in the world, Peter. Do you

90

know that? You're the only one I can trust. You're
the only one in the world that understands."

"Close your eyes!" Peter said. "Please. Shut up
and close your eyes. Don't talk any more, Chad. Just
don't talk."

He waited there in the wood, watching as Chad
Kimberley approached him. He waited while Chad's
arms went around him and drew him close.

"You're the first, Peter. You're my only friend so
you're the first. And now we must go."

Peter Bell screamed out loud and he tore free.
"Granny was right!" he cried. "He was right. You
are crazy." He moved away, backward, stumbling,
saying it again and again. You're crazy, Chad.
You're crazy." He retreated, saying it, retreated
until all he could see were Chad Kimberley's eyes,
glowing, staring after him. Then he cried it one
final time and turned, running, circling deeper into
the wood. . . .

His arms were hugging a giant pine and he was
staring at the moon. The fragrance of pine hung
thick in the air; a gentle breeze blew in from the
lake, stirring the pine needles into aimless movement. His throat ached and his eyes burned, so he
closed them and hugged the tree more tightly, feeling his heart beat. There had to be something, he
told himself, something he could do, some course
to follow. He opened one eye and sighted up along
the mammoth tree trunk, staring through the clustered branches at the clustered stars. There had to
be something. There had to be. He knew that.
Finally he remembered the fifty-dollar bill and then
he began to run again. . . .

When he reached the cottage he twisted the door
handle and threw his weight against the door. It was
locked. He clenched both fists and began pounding,

feeling the door shake. The catch started to loosen so he hit harder, his hands stinging, shouting her name with his dry mouth. The door rattled, then opened a crack. He drove against it, forcing her backward into the room. She watched him, eyes bright, her great white towel draped around her body.

"Here," Peter said. "Here," and he walked into the cottage and held the money out to her.

She stepped away, still watching him. "Get out," she whispered.

"I won't," he said. His throat hurt him when he talked so he stopped and tried to swallow. "I'm staying here."

"Get out," she whispered again. "Get out."

"There's no reason for me to. I know everything now."

"You better shut up. You better not say any more."

"Here," and he reached out again, the bill crumpled in his hand. "I've got the money. Isn't that the way it works? Here. Take it. It's fifty dollars. That's a lot for someone like you."

"Shut up!" Tillie said again, her voice rising. "Don't you go calling me names. Don't you ever call me names. You rich bastard. Who do you think you are? What the hell did you ever do to get rich? You just got born in the right place. Well, I didn't. I got born in the wrong place but that doesn't mean I got to stay there. So you better sit on your money. You better sit on it tight, because I'm coming." She was screaming at him across the darkened room, her voice shaking more and more until it broke. They stared at each other through the darkness and he was amazed to see that she was crying, her body trembling, her mouth opening and closing but without sound.

Then she let go of the towel and it fell away from her. Her breasts were white, and her eyes glistened. "Here," she whispered. "Is this what you wanted? Is this what you came for? Are you happy now?"

"No," Peter said softly. "No."

"Then why did you come? Why did you have to come? Why couldn't you just leave me alone?" She began walking slowly toward him.

He did not move.

"Why?" she whispered. "Why? You were the only one that didn't know. I never wanted you to know. So why did you have to come?" She stood in front of him, crying harder. Then she ducked her head and fell against him. He could feel her tears wet against his shirt. "Why?" she whispered. "Why?"

"I loved you," he mumbled, his arms hanging loosely at his sides. "That's what I was trying to tell you. Tonight. Out on the lake. That I loved you. I swear to God I did."

She took his hand and led him through the darkness to her bed. "You poor bastard," she whispered. Together they lay down. Then he put his arms around her and closed his eyes. . . .

He knew it was day. Through the window on the opposite wall of the cottage, the crisscrossing of branches became gradually visible, a purple maze of branches melding into the purple sky beyond. The sun had not yet risen. But it was day.

Peter Bell sat up in bed and rubbed his eyes. Beside him Tillie stirred. Gently he reached out and touched her skin, his hand moving slowly across her warm, tanned shoulder. Quietly, trying not to wake her, he bent down and kissed her auburn hair. Her eyes half open, she folded her arms around his neck, bringing his head down until their lips met. She dropped her arms lazily. He kissed her one more time.

He was almost fully dressed when she stirred again, her eyes fully open now, watching him. "What are you doing?" she said, sitting up, pulling the sheet around her.

"I've got to go," he whispered. "I didn't mean to wake you. I'm sorry."

"What time is it?"

"I don't know. Early." He walked over to her and held out the fifty-dollar bill. "Here, Tillie," he said. "I want you to have this."

She pushed his hand away. "I don't want it."

"Take it anyway. Please. I really want you to have it. Please. Take it."

She shook her head.

"I'm going to leave it here on the table," he said, and he put it down. Then he started for the door.

She jumped up, holding the white sheet around her. Moving quickly to the table, she grabbed the money and crumpled it in her hand. "I told you I wasn't going to take it."

He opened the door. "And I told you I wanted you to."

She threw the money toward him. It dropped noiselessly to the ground outside. He looked down at it.

"Pick it up," Tillie said.

"No."

"I'm just going to leave it there then."

"All right," he said. "You do whatever you want."

She hurried to the doorway. "I'm not kidding."

"Neither am I," and he took a step backward, his eyes still on her.

She moved away from the money into the cottage.

"Pick it up."

"No."

He took another step. He could no longer see her face clearly; she stood in shadow.

"Pick it up."

"No." Another step.

"You better."

"I won't."

She was against the far wall of the cottage now and he was standing on the edge of the dusty road, the money lying on the ground between them.

"I'm telling you for the last time," she yelled. "I mean it."

He backed onto the road, able only to see the vague white outline of the sheet as she stood pressed against the far wall of the cottage. "I'm going, Tillie," he called. "Good-bye." She did not answer. "Good-bye," he called again. And then a third time, "Good-bye." With that he turned and started running up the hill.

Cabin number six was empty so he did not bother going inside. He hurried on to Chad's cabin and opened the door. It was empty. The bed had not been slept in. Spinning around, he headed for The Lodge. There was no one there. He stood in the center of the hallway and started calling up the stairs. "Chad," he called. "Chad." There was no reply. He yelled the name again. "Chad!" and waited. Still nothing. He turned and banged through the front door, racing across the lawn to cabin number one.

Granny was asleep. He lay on his back, breathing

deeply, his face covered with a light film of perspiration.

"Granny," Peter said sharply. "Granny, get up."

Granny sat, eyes wide, staring.

"Where's Chad?"

Granny shook his head.

"Where's Chad?" Peter said again.

"I don't know. Isn't he in his cabin?"

"No, he isn't in his cabin. Where do you think he is?"

Granny stood. "I don't know. I don't know. Is something wrong?"

"Pray," Peter said, and he left.

He stood in the center of the lawn, turning around and around, calling. There was no answer. He called again and waited. No answer. Then he stopped. "Chad's in the clearing," he said out loud. "He's in the clearing," and he began running again.

He raced down the hill to the lake and then into the purple wood, the low-hanging branches snapping out at his face, stinging him, but he did not stop. His breath was short and his chest burned from running but he kept on, his hands clenched, his elbows bent, tucked into his body. Up ahead he saw the grove of birch and he slowed, slipping in and out between the trees. At the edge of the grove he stopped.

The clearing was empty.

Nodding, Peter walked to the tree stump and sat down. He put his head in his hands and closed his eyes, hearing nothing but the sound of his own breathing. His body began to shake but he fought it off, calming himself as best he could. He had known all along where Chad was. Now there was nothing left to do but go and get him.

Pushing himself to his feet, he began to walk.

There was no point in running any more; the time for that was over. And as he walked his mind traveled back to another day, years before, to a beautiful summer afternoon. He was playing on the beach below his house, skipping stones into the rough green water of Lake Michigan. At the top of the bluff, on the edge of the lawn, he saw his father standing. "Peter!" Jacob had called. "Peter!" And he had dropped his handful of stones and started up the bluff. "Hurry, Peter," Jacob had called. "Run, Peter, run." But he had not run. The time for that was over. He knew somehow that his mother had died, that the damage had been done.

So he walked. He walked through the trees, through the maze of birch and pine. He walked up the hill that led toward camp. He walked past The Lodge and the cabins, past the tennis courts, down the hill toward the baseball diamond. But he did not stop when he reached it. He continued on slowly. The time for running was over; the damage had been done.

So he walked. And as he walked he seemed to be suddenly conscious of everything, of all the changes that were going on around him. His senses seemed extraordinarily alert. He could taste the wet dawn air. He could smell the dew rising from the wet grass, turning slowly into mist. He saw the sun flaming, beginning to rise above the red horizon. He stared at the sun, forced his eyes into focusing on it in spite of its brightness. His eyes began to water but he would not allow them to look away; he kept on staring at the sun. He could hear everything, all the morning sounds; birds and squirrels and from somewhere, faintly, a distant bell. The sun was brighter now, higher, one quarter visible. The mist began to fade from the edge of the red horizon.

He slowed. Off to his left a rabbit darted across the grass, scurrying into the safety of the wood. He stopped. The sun felt hotter than before.. He was perspiring terribly and he began to think that he was walking toward the sun, that it was his destination, that he could only rest when he had stepped inside the flames. Peter shook his head, blinking. He closed his eyes and looked away from the sun. His legs would not move. He commanded them and finally, grudgingly, they obeyed him, and he was walking again, very slowly now, getting nearer, nearer.

Then he was there.

He stood for a moment on the edge of the council ring. The sun was at his back but he could still feel the flames burning his face. That was his only sensation. Heat. He took a step forward, fighting to maintain control. Another step. A third.

Chad Kimberley was nailed to the cross. He stood on the ground, a single thick nail protruding from each of his bare feet. There was a third nail sticking through his left hand, and a thin line of red trailed down his palm. His right hand was clear, unmarked, but he held it straight out, pressing it against the wooden crosspiece. His eyes were closed; his head hung limply to one side.

"Chad!" Peter said, and his steps quickened until he was running across the council ring.

Chad Kimberley opened his eyes, and he stared blankly for a moment. Then somehow he smiled. "Peter," he whispered. "Peter. I knew you'd come. I knew you'd come when I needed you. I knew it, Peter. You're my only friend, and I knew you'd come."

He allowed his right arm to drop, palm open. Peter followed the gesture with his eyes. A rock and a fourth nail lay at Chad's feet. Slowly, in agony, he raised his arm and pressed it back against the wooden crosspiece.

"Nail me to the cross, Peter. Nail me to the cross." Peter Bell dropped to his knees and began clawing at the nails, trying to pull them out of the bruised, bloody feet. "Nail me to the cross, Peter." The first nail came free. "Help me, Peter. Nail me to the cross." The second nail came free. He stood and reached up for the left hand. "Help me, Peter. Help me. Nail me to the cross." It was a chant now and he tried not to listen. "Nail me to the cross, Peter. Nail me to the cross." He picked at the nail that stuck through the broken left hand of Chad Kimberley. "Nail me to the cross, Peter. Nail me to the cross." The nail was in too deeply; there was nothing he could do. He began slamming his fists against the wooden crosspiece, but it was no use. "Nail me to the cross, Peter. Nail me to the cross." Screaming now. "Nail me to the cross, Peter! Nail me to the cross!" He bent down and grabbed the rock and smashed it against the back of the wooden crosspiece, where the tip of the nail stuck out. He hit it again and again and finally he was able to reach up and tuck his fingers under the nail head and pull it through the left hand of Chad Kimberley.

The arm dropped limply. Chad looked at it for just a moment. Then he screamed one final time and his beautiful face fell apart and he dropped like a stone into the waiting arms of Peter Bell....

xi

THERE WERE THREE OF THEM standing by the railroad tracks. It was an hour or so later, but the sun was already hot and they were perspiring heavily as they stood alongside the camp station wagon, waiting for the train.

"It's a terrible thing," Jeff was saying. He dried his palms with his handkerchief, a thick stocky man, muscular, baby-faced. "A terrible thing."

Granny nodded.

Peter Bell said nothing, but stared instead down the visible mile of track. The train was already five minutes late, and still there was no sign.

"I don't know," Jeff went on. "I've been thinking about it. Maybe it was my fault. Maybe if I'd come back a couple of days earlier. Maybe if I'd been . . ."

"It wasn't your fault," Granny cut in. "It was the doctors'. They let him out too soon. He wasn't fit to be out. He would have cracked up anyway. No matter who'd been here."

"Maybe so," Jeff nodded. "But it's a terrible thing all the same." He turned to Peter Bell. "Most terrible thing ever happened up here. By far. Wouldn't you say so?"

"I wouldn't know," Peter answered.

"Well, Jesus, man," Jeff said. "Can you imagine anything worse? I mean, it's not the kind of thing that goes on up here every day. There's never been anything like it before. It's sure as hell not typical of what goes on up here. You'd say that, wouldn't you?"

"I wouldn't know," Peter said again.

"What I'm saying," Jeff confided, lowering his voice. "What I'm saying is just that I don't see any point to spreading the news around, do you? I mean, it's like Granny said. The doctors let him out too soon. It could have happened anyplace. So I don't see how it's going to do anybody any good spreading it around."

"I won't spread it around," Peter muttered. "You can relax."

"I wonder where the hell that train is," Jeff said, and he sauntered away down the track, shading his eyes from the sun.

Granny came over and stood beside Peter. "I just wanted you to know that I'm sorry," he said.

"Sure you are," Peter answered.

Granny ran his hands across the front of his T-shirt. "I am," he went on. "I didn't mean for this to happen. The joke part, sure. I meant that. But that was all."

Peter turned and began to walk but Granny grabbed him and spun him around. "Get your hands off me," Peter said. "Right now. And I'm not kidding."

Granny held on. "I just want to make sure you understand," he said. "I just want . . ."

"I understand," Peter cut in, tearing free. "I understand. You're scared, that's all."

Granny laughed. "Scared? Of what?"

"You'll get yours someday," Peter whispered. "I swear to God you'll get yours."

Again the laugh. "Yeah? Who's going to give it to me?"

Jeff sauntered back. "Train's coming," he said. "Better get him out of the car."

They opened the rear door of the station wagon. "Easy with him," Jeff said. "Easy with him."

Granny reached inside. "I'll get him, Jeff."

"His name is Chad!" Peter yelled suddenly. "Not 'him.' Chad!" The sound of the engine grew louder. "Now get away. Both of you get away and let me do it." He pushed between them and took Chad Kimberley by his unbandaged hand and carefully led him out. Chad stood straight, staring ahead.

"I'll wire both your fathers as soon as I get back to camp," Jeff said. "They'll meet the train."

Peter began leading Chad up the embankment toward the tracks.

"Easy with him," Jeff cautioned. "He's not walking so good yet." The sound of the engine grew louder. "So long now," Jeff went on. "And explain to the Kimberleys how I feel about it. Tell them I'll write them a letter first chance I get."

Peter whirled. "You don't care!" he shouted

down at them. "You don't care! Neither of you care!"

" 'Course I care," Jeff answered. "But it's done now. There's no point in spreading it around. It's not going to do anybody any good. We agreed on that, didn't we?"

The train slowed in front of them. Peter turned Chad away from the track and spread his hand over Chad's open eyes. The trained stopped. He led Chad to the steps. From above a conductor watched them.

"So long, boy," Jeff shouted, waving. "Have a good trip now."

They mounted the steps. The train started again, picking up speed, faster and faster. It roared along the rim of Lake Cherokee, and in the distance Peter could see the empty camp dock protruding out into the water. He watched for a moment until the lake blurred into a forest of pine. Then Camp Blackpine Camp for Boys lay behind him.

Taking Chad by the hand, Peter followed the conductor along the corridor to their room. "Is there anything I can do?" the conductor asked. "Is your friend all right?"

"He's fine," Peter answered, opening the door. "He's fine now. He's going home."

Closing the door, he led Chad to a seat by the window and gently guided him down. Chad sat rigidly, staring straight ahead. "Look out the window," Peter whispered. "It's pretty out there." Chad stared straight ahead. Kneeling, Peter removed the bedroom slippers from the swollen bandaged feet of Chad Kimberley. He stood. "You'll be more comfortable now," he said. "Is your hand all right?" He looked down at the bandaged palm, at the four pink fingers sticking through. Chad stared straight ahead. There was no sound at all in the stuffy rectangular room. "Are you too warm, Chad? Is it too warm in here for you?" There was no answer. "Are you hungry? Can I get you some food?" There was no answer. "How would you like me to read to you?" No answer. Chad Kimberley stared straight ahead, his blue eyes wide, unblinking. "Maybe some sleep, then. Close your eyes, Chad." Peter pulled down the dark green shades. Sunlight streaked in through the window edges, striping the semidarkened room. "Close your eyes, Chad," he whispered again. "Close your eyes and go to sleep." The eyes stayed open. "O.K.," Peter whispered. "You do what you want. I'm going to read." He sat down on the bench opposite and switched on the lamp. Taking a paper-backed book from his pocket, he opened it to the first page. Then he glanced up. Chad's eyes were staring at him. Peter inched down the bench, out of the stare. The eyes did not follow. He began to read. He read the opening line and then the opening paragraph and then he glanced up again. Chad's eyes were still open, still staring. Peter dropped the book on the bench beside him and stood.

"You've got to close your eyes, Chad," he whispered. "Please. Come on. You've just got to." The eyes stayed open. Peter walked to the door. "I'm going to get something to eat," he said. "Do you want me to bring you anything?" No answer. He opened the door. "You stay here, then. Stay right here. I won't be long. O.K.?" No answer; nothing. Peter stepped out into the corridor and closed the door. Then he began to walk slowly through the car in the direction of the diner.

The dining car was full and there was a line of people waiting, so he took his place at the end of it. The line moved very slowly; he watched the Negro waiters scurrying back and forth along the aisle. He realized that he wasn't hungry but he did not move. He stayed in place at the end of the line, watching the waiters and the other people in the car.

When his turn came he sat down by himself and ordered breakfast. He ordered ham and eggs and they came quickly, so he dawdled over them, picking at them with the tines of his fork until they were cold. Then he ordered a cup of coffee and waited until it was cold. He ordered another cup of coffee, leaving it untouched in front of him.

He knew what was happening to him and he leaned back and shut his eyes. Finally he paid the waiter and left. He walked slowly through the train. When he reached his room he stopped and quietly opened the door.

Chad had not moved. His hands folded in his lap, the bandaged one on top, he stared straight ahead. Peter closed the door and started walking up and down the corridor, his hands jammed in his pockets. People passed him and he pressed his face against the cold metal side of the car, sucking in his breath, holding it until his chest ached. Then, when he could no longer control the shaking of his body, he walked into the room.

"I'm back," he said. No answer. Peter reached out and lifted the shades, flooding the room with light. Chad did not blink. Peter sat down on the bench and picked up his book. He held it a moment, then ripped it in two, viciously, snapping it.

"Close your eyes," he said louder. "And I'm not asking you now, Chad, I'm telling you. Close your eyes." He reached across the warm room and placed his fingertips on Chad's eyelids. But he did not push them down.

He had known it was coming for a long time, so he was not surprised when the tears splashed down his face. He almost welcomed them as he dropped to the floor and wept; Peter Bell, on his knees, crying at last. He crawled forward until he could lock his arms around Chad Kimberley's legs, until he could press his face down onto Chad's knees. He stayed that way, sobbing, his body shaking terribly, the words forming inside him, beginning to force their way from his throat.

"I don't care either, Chad," he sobbed. "I don't care. Do you hear me? I don't care. I don't care. I'm sorry but I don't care, I don't care. I don't care. I don't care...."

xii

It was dusk when the train reached Athens.

Through the dirt-smeared window, Peter could see them waiting, his father and the Kimberleys. The Kimberleys stood close to one another beneath the yellow light; his father stood a few feet away, his hands behind his back, rocking, rocking.

The train slowed. Peter stood up. "Come on, Chad," he said. Chad did not move. "Come on," Peter said again, and he clapped his hands together sharply, the sound suddenly filling the quiet room. "Now, Chad! Get up!" Still no movement.

Reaching down, he took Chad by the hand and pulled him to his feet. Peter led the way as they moved slowly, hand in hand, out of the room, along the corridor to the end of the car. The conductor opened the door for them, watching as they crept along.

The train stopped. Peter walked down the steps backward, leading Chad, gently guiding him, making sure that he did not fall. When they stood on the station platform, he released Chad's hand and nodded to the conductor. The train began to move.

The rest was a dumb show. Peter seemed aware only of movement, not of sound. Patterns began to form. First there was nothing. Then the Kimberleys took a step forward. Peter waited alongside Chad. The Kimberleys took another step. Then a third. Then they were running. Peter backed away from Chad. The Kimberleys rushed at their son, stopping only after they had flanked him, one on each side, all three of them pale yellow in the yellow dusk. The Kimberleys started to move again, but Chad remained motionless. They came back to him, took him by the hand. Then they led him away, quickly, toward the parking lot. Peter watched them until they were out of sight. He was suddenly conscious of his father standing alongside him. They looked at each other.

"Helluva short summer," Jacob Bell said.

Peter nodded, and together they started off in the same direction the Kimberleys had taken. As they approached Peter saw them driving away. They were all in the front seat, Chad in the middle, his head stiff and straight, his eyes staring.

"What happened?" Jacob asked finally.

"I don't know," Peter muttered. "A lot."

"You feel like telling me about it?"

They got into the car. Peter slumped back against the seat, his eyes open, staring through the windshield at the red taillights disappearing in the darkness. "Tell you about it?" He closed his eyes; the Kimberleys were gone. "I don't know if I can."

"You want to try?"

"Yes," Peter nodded. "Yes, I do." He felt suddenly very tired, but he began to talk, softly, "Everything went fine in the beginning," he whispered. "The train trip, I mean. I got up there in the morning. It was a beautiful day, and..." So he talked. He talked while they drove home. He talked while Bertha fed him supper. He talked after that as he and his father strolled along the quiet beach below their house. He talked on and on, omitting nothing, pouring it all out. And as he talked his body began to drain. His eyes burned and he ached and his throat felt dry. But he talked until he was done. He was back up in his own room by that time, in his own bed, lying flat, staring at the ceiling, his father sitting close beside him.

When he was finished, he stopped.

Jacob stood. "Don't go away," he said, and he disappeared, returning a moment later with a glass of water. "Here," he said. "Take these," and he handed Peter two sleeping pills. "Not that I figure you got much use of them. But take them anyway."

Peter sat up, swallowed the pills, and lay down again. Jacob turned out the lights. The room was cool and very dark; a soft wind blew in from the shore of Lake Michigan.

"What do you think?" Peter asked finally.

"Well," Jacob said, after a pause. "I can't give you no sympathy."

"I'm not asking for it."

"Sure you are. But I can't give you any. And I'll tell you why. Because you're so God damned lucky just being young that no matter what happens it's gravy."

There was no sound in the room; the wind puffed noiselessly at the curtains by the windows. Beyond, the sky was dark; there was no moon. Peter lay quietly, his father still beside him. His legs felt empty, completely drained, and his eyes were heavy so that he had to fight to keep them open.

Jacob stood. "Relax," he whispered. "Go to sleep."

"No." Peter pushed himself up onto his elbows. "No. I'm not ready to go to sleep. I can't go to sleep yet." He tried tensing his empty body but he could not. "I can't go to sleep yet."

"Three to one you do."

"No," Peter said, his voice louder. "Don't you understand? I can't get to sleep yet. I can't."

"And why can't you?"

"I've got to wait. Don't you understand?" His arms could no longer support his body and he fell back, struggling to keep his eyes open. "I'm waiting for something to happen. Don't you see? Chad went to the cross and I'm waiting for something to happen. I'm waiting for something to happen. I'm..."

He could feel himself drifting away, farther and farther away, but he thought it over and over in his mind. "I'm waiting for something to happen. I'm waiting for something to happen."

He heard his father leaving, and he yelled out loud, "Don't." Then his father's voice, softly, from some great distance.

"Sleep it off, you poor bastard. Sleep it off."

He was drifting again. Faster now. Everything was rushing past him. But there was something. He had heard it before. And then he remembered. Tillie. Tillie standing in front of him, the white

110

towel falling away. He could see her; he could see her tanned shoulders and her white breasts and the white towel falling away. So he dreamed of Tillie. And oh God, oh my God, oh my Jesus God, it was a beautiful dream....

xiii

I'VE DREAMED a decade's worth of dreams since that anticlimactic evening, but none of them seems so remote to me now as does Peter Bell himself. We seem so different, he and I, that there are times, moments when I allow myself to indulge in the luxury of memory, that I must consciously break the flow of images and concentrate, trying to separate my own past from a flood of fiction. Did he do that? Or did I read about it? Was it Peter Bell who lay rigid in the clearing, or was it...? Did he pull the green canoe across the moonlit lake, or...? The memories shift and fade, illusory, darting out from a hidden corner of my mind, racing for new shelter, daring me almost to catch them.

I cannot reconcile the "he" with the "I." Certainly, I lack his ungainly interests, his ceaseless, savage curiosity. I don't ask many questions any more. My world is quiet now; I keep it that way, and good or bad at least it is my own. But occasionally he does come back to me, encroaching, forcing me into remembering him, into acknowledging that, no matter how much I want to kill him, I cannot. He continues to intrude; just last week I saw Tillie Keck's picture in the newspaper.

I had slept well into the morning, and when I got downstairs Bertha began chiding me as she went about heating up some coffee. I chatted with her, back and forth, thumbing through the Saturday *Tribune*. I was in the act of turning to a new page when I saw her picture.

Quickly I read the article. It was comparatively brief, stating simply that Tillie—she was referred to by a different name, but I have forgotten it—had married a rather chinless young man who happened to be the heir to a Bolivian tin fortune. Tillie, it said, was a model. She appeared to be thinner than ten years before, her face sharper in plane, but, all in all, she was still very beautiful. I ripped the picture from the paper, yelled for Bertha to forget the coffee, and hurried upstairs, putting on a bathing suit. Then I rummaged through the attic until I found the baseball.

Walking outside, I nodded good morning to Jacob, who lay dozing in a contour chair, an unlit cigar in his mouth. I continued on by him, down the bluff to the beach. The sun was already hot, and I was perspiring slightly as I walked to the edge of the water and sat down.

Still in something of a morning haze, I blew the dust from the baseball, turning it in my hands until

113

I saw the autograph. "To Peter. Good luck from Joe DiMaggio." I placed my fingers over the signature and shifted the ball from one hand to the other, playing a solitary shell game.

Finally I dropped it onto the warm sand and picked up the picture of Tillie, staring at it, smoothing it against my leg. Bringing it close to my eyes, I held it at various angles, staring, shaking my head, trying to think. What had she been wearing that first day in the drugstore? Green? Was her skirt green? I could see it swirling around her tanned legs as she walked; I felt her body touching mine as I held the door open for her. It must have been green. And her sleeveless blouse was white. White was a good color for her. I had told her that.

I put the paper on the sand beside me. In a moment the wind was picking at it, jabbing, curling the corners. I started to reach for it but stopped, watching instead as the wind lifted it, whirling it into the air. In a moment it came down again onto the sand, skittering on edge, rolling, rolling. Then the wind had it a second time, pulling it upward, finally slapping it down on top of the lake. It smoothed out then, quietly floating, a paper sailboat without a sail. I sat watching it, wondering if Granny had also found the picture, wondering if he remembered.

I see him occasionally. At the country club or speeding around town in some blatantly expensive foreign car. He is almost completely bald now and tending slightly to flesh. He drinks a great deal; I have seen him drunk many times. For, as I predicted ten years earlier, Granny got his. He married a girl whose breasts are too big.

Originally, when he married her, she was an olive-skinned full-blown girl from the Main Line outside

114

Philadelphia. She was voluptuous then, a sensuous thing, and all eyes turned to follow her as she moved. But her body never fully recovered from the ordeal of their first child, and now her breasts are too big. It embarrasses Granny to be seen with her, and I mention that with undisguised bad will. She bounces. And she isn't voluptuous any more.

Chad I saw often. When I went East to college I used to visit him in Vermont, and we would walk around the sanitarium grounds, chatting on about inconsequentials. He seemed fine, at least to me. But then he always did; I could never see far beyond his smile. I have no clear recollection of any of our visits. They were all similar, all superficial, all, I fear, a trifle dull. He stayed in Vermont for several years, finally being transferred to a somewhat more relaxed institution in Arizona. We corresponded, and once when he was allowed to come home for Christmas, we had a farewell drink together.

Shortly afterward he disappeared. There are many rumors. That he has been permanently put away; that he has gone to live in Europe; that he committed suicide. I have never presumed to ask the Kimberleys point-blank about it; probably they don't know either. But I do have my own thoughts on the subject. I picture him somewhere in the Orient. He is clad in a loincloth, sitting hunched on the eastern side of some gently sloping hill. His skin is black, his hair bleached white, and he is sitting quietly, waiting for the sun to rise. That, as I said, is my own idea; no one knows for sure ...

I lay back on the sand. It had turned into an agonizingly beautiful morning; the sun was hot but the wind cooled me and I lay still, caught comfortably between the two. I relaxed, listening to the steady rhythmic slapping of the waves against the shore. I closed my eyes, drifting, and suddenly the room was filled with children, most of them crying, and I could hear the click of castanets, growing louder and louder. Then the bald piano player began to play in rhythm with the clicking, and the two lines began to move.

And so it's your turn to curtsy, my turn to bow, your turn to curtsy, now mine, you, now me, on and on, until one of the dancers falls, I suppose, or until the dance is ended....

William Goldman

is also the author of

Boys & Girls Together

the scorching new bestseller
coming soon from
Corgi Books!!!

A SELECTION OF FINE READING AVAILABLE IN CORGI BOOKS

Novels

☐ FG	1541	MAN AND SEX	*Joseph F. Kaufman, M.D., and Griffith Borgeson*	5/–
☐ BG	7331	THE DISPOSSESSED—a study of the sex-life of Bantu women	*Laura Longmore*	8/6
☐ GC	7314	WRESTLING (illustrated)	*David Marchbanks*	3/6
☐ FG	7215	TENPIN BOWLING (illustrated)	*John Moyes*	5/–
☐ FG	7277	THE CORGI SPORTS ALMANAC	*Compiled by Tom Owen*	5/–
☐ FG	7248	WISDOM OF THE ANCIENTS	*T. Lobsang Rampa*	5/–
☐ FG	7349	THE SAFFRON ROBE	*T. Lobsang Rampa*	5/–

Westerns

☐ GW	7310	TO THE LAST MAN	*Zane Grey*	3/6
☐ GW	7344	THE THUNDERING HERD	*Zane Grey*	3/6
☐ GW	7345	THE KEY-LOCK MAN	*Louis L'Amour*	3/6
☐ GW	7293	THE SACKETT BRAND	*Louis L'Amour*	3/6
☐ GW	7362	JOHNNY NELSON	*Clarence E. Mulford*	3/6
☐ GW	7294	THE MAN FROM BAR-20	*Clarence E. Mulford*	3/6
☐ GW	7274	SHANE	*Jack Schaefer*	3/6
☐ GW	7328	DESERT CROSSING	*Luke Short*	3/6
☐ GW	7363	SUMMER OF THE SMOKE	*Luke Short*	3/6
☐ GW	7275	SUDDEN PLAYS A HAND	*Oliver Strange*	3/6
☐ GW	7276	THE RANGE ROBBERS	*Oliver Strange*	3/6

Crime

☐ GC	7342	FLASHPOINT	*Jean Bruce*	3/6
☐ GC	7309	LADY, THIS IS MURDER	*Peter Chambers*	3/6
☐ GC	7324	THE SPEAKER	*John Creasey*	3/6
☐ GC	7308	THE BARON RETURNS	*John Creasey*	3/6
☐ GC	7359	BLACK FOR THE BARON	*John Creasey*	3/6
☐ GC	7292	SPILL THE JACKPOT	*A. A. Fair (Erle Stanley Gardner)*	3/6
☐ GC	7325	FISH OR CUT BAIT	*A. A. Fair*	3/6
☐ GC	7224	THE LIQUIDATOR	*John Gardner*	3/6
☐ GC	7347	THAT DARN CAT	*The Gordons*	3/6
☐ GC	7341	THE MAN WHO SOLD DEATH	*James Munro*	3/6
☐ GC	7307	THE SNAKE	*Mickey Spillane*	3/6
☐ GC	7202	KILLER MINE	*Mickey Spillane*	3/6
☐ GC	7360	DEATH OF A NUDE	*Douglas Warner*	3/6

*All these great books are available at your local bookshop or newsagent; or can be ordered
direct from the publisher. Just tick the titles you wont and fill in the form below.*

— — — — — — — — — — — — — — — —

CORGI BOOKS, Cash Sales Department, Bashley Road, London, N.W.10.
Please send cheque or postal order. No currency, PLEASE. Allow 6d. per book to
cover the cost of postage on orders of less than 6 books.

NAME ....

ADDRESS ....

(MAR. 66) ....